SILVER DREAMS

SILVER DREAMS

A MYTH *of* THE SIXTH SENSE

JOYCE PETSCHEK

ILLUSTRATIONS BY STEPHEN SNELL

CELESTIAL ARTS
BERKELEY, CALIFORNIA

CELESTIAL ARTS
P.O. Box 7327
Berkeley, California 94707

Cover art and interior illustrations by Stephen Snell
Cover and text design by Ken Scott
Production by David Charlsen

Library of Congress Catalog Card Number: 90-82143

FIRST EDITION

0 9 8 7 6 5 4 3 2 1
94 93 92 91 90

Printed in Hong Kong

To Michael
(Number One of Nebulae)

CONTENTS

Contents

"There is always something more to discover. Seeking never ends."

"The individual way is a peculiar serpentine way,
and that is the way of the dream."

CARL GUSTAV JUNG
October 1929, Zurich

· I ·

SERPENTINE SHADOWS

I T WAS ONE OF THOSE MORNINGS when nothing felt right. The quiet dawn held an air of apprehension as some strange anxiety invaded the stillness of my bedroom. Its pulsations crept under the door, seeped into the walls, crawled across the ceiling. Cowering beneath the bed covers, the voice inside my head screamed: "What's going on? What's happening?" My body tense from troubled thoughts, my searching eyes probed the surrounding silence. Only then did my laser beam mind penetrate my parents' bedroom walls. "There they go again!" the voice inside my head proclaimed. Their anger, seething from years of suspicion, had erupted anew.

How my frightened thoughts jammed together! My body yearned to melt into the mattress, my psyche dreaded the coming day. Accused Father would disappear. Angry Mother would unleash her frustrations on me. Her familiar speech pounded through my head, "Aisling, come here this very minute!" "Aisling, why did you do that?" "Aisling, why don't you ever listen?" Clenched teeth raged in revolt, no part of me stirred from my four-poster bed. Feelings turned numb, as crumpled white pillows covered my rising tears. How I longed to flee the trauma of home!

Yet teenage tensions seemed no different from childhood chaos, except now, even my dreams were disillusioned. No longer did a golden hand tap my shoulder. No blue fairies danced upon bedroom walls. No voice whispered, "Aisling, Aisling, you are chosen! You are chosen!" No Silver Bird enticed me onto his soothing wings. Wisdom words from Whisper could no longer comfort my trembling thoughts. "Trust, trust, that you must!" seemed a lifetime ago. No visions of escape could calm my inner turmoil. A teenager did not want the Wise Old Woman to say, "My, my how you've grown!" Yet, why did the Old Man of the Universe hover about? How he kept repeating, "There is always something more to discover. Seeking never ends." With sickle in hand and a twinkle in his eye, he offered oppor-

1

tunities beyond the trauma of home. "I am the Guardian of your Universe, the Keeper of Time, the Doorway to Space, the Gateway through the Sun into the Galaxy." His measured words kept urging me forward. Time exploded in directions beyond my control, and *signs of the zodiac* replaced the *hands of the clock*. With infinite patience, again and again, the Old Man would say, "Now, continue your Quest, for it never ends."

Yet such sentiment disturbed my adolescent feelings. Fear loomed far stronger than the fantasy of freedom. Parental quarrels had become painful events. Even my four-poster bed, with its quilt of gigantic red roses and white organdy curtains, offered little consolation. Fright lay behind this mask of sweetness. Desperate feelings of wanting to run, not knowing where to go, where to hide. Everything mean and malicious now surfaced. My dressing table mirror reflected a face of sadness, and voices tormented me with mocking words. "Aisling, Aisling! You don't belong anywhere! You're not loved by anyone! You're invisible! Even to yourself!" Passionately did my innocence argue, defend my goodness, my goddess within.

Rebellion gave me the courage to act. No longer would my anger retreat in resentment. Anxiety could not be avoided. For I, Aisling, was sixteen years old. Fragile from the chaos of conflict, my stifled feelings were ready to burst. Thoughts of mutiny consumed my mind. Mother's demands had to be confronted. My distress had to defend my position. How I yearned for attention, how I wanted to belong. How I needed to be noticed. For neither Mother nor Father honored my feelings, heeded my emotions, nor heard my words.

Newly erupted passions announced this revolt as my temper exploded beyond belief. Mother would lament, "What happened to my sweet little girl?" Father, silent and steadfast, would stare, shake his head and silently leave the room. How he reminded me of the Keeper of Time, forever disappearing, never around when trouble began. The scene was always the same. Mother would rage. The household would declare that I, Aisling, had destroyed the *peace* of home. My brother would torment me, chase my frantic feet down stone paths, dangle green garden snakes. Then did my tunnel eyes narrow, pierce his evil ways. "Watch out! Just you wait! The black witch will demolish you yet!"

As resentment released itself, my inner voices called: "Aisling, fight for your feelings! Go for your life! Now and forever!" Then did my volcanic temper erupt. My mind felt powerful, my body free of frustration! Yet no one could fathom what would tilt my emotional scale. Only when frightened did such turmoil torment me. Then feelings of futility made my heart hesitate. Swallowed words stuck in my throat. I would mutter "yes" instead of "no", tears flooding my face. Stifled anger left me depressed, fright silenced my tongue. Yet frustration forced me forward, and mounting tensions made my fury rise.

As emotions shattered, so inner voices enticed and encouraged. "Speak up, Aisling! Do not hesitate now! Your Fate dangles by a thread!" How my anxiety raced beyond present time! Words of wisdom filled my thoughts. Familiar scenes flashed before my eyes, memories my mind would not erase. How such scenes comforted my churning heart! Then did potential loom beyond parental tensions. Forgotten words of Whisper would be heard. "Trusting is not knowing where you are going! Faith is the path of heart!" "Free will is whether you listen to your inner *or* outer voice." "The path, the path, follow the path!" "Within the dark, you'll find the light!" Had these words of Whisper now become *me* talking to myself?

Yet challenge also brought doubt. My adolescent awareness questioned *where* and *why* such thoughts arose. Travels beyond *time* left me consumed with confusion. My imagination felt both frazzled and free. How often, returning from flights of fantasy, did my surroundings seem foreign. Always something besides these bizarre scenes bothered me. Was it my teenage yearning to be *real*? My unwillingness to exist only in a world of *dreams*? Such moments of doubt brought the Keeper of Time. Then would he speak of spirals, "the spinning outwards, the whirling around and around, the confusion before the calmness of the tranquil center."

Yet my body resisted whatever changes were coming, and my mind rejected Whisper's childhood words: "Life is taking chances. Chances are changes." Instead, school studies consumed my silent thoughts. Psychic barriers kept potential friends away and my bedroom became a retreat for reflection. Safe from suspicious eyes, its privacy protected me. Yellow and blue porcelain cats guarded my locked door. Then were countless pages read, poetry scribbled, private notes tucked within precious books. Hidden in my antique desk, my diary held visions of wishes and wants. Daydreams became the mistress of my mind. Curled in my red chintz chair, my tunnel eyes would gaze beyond the garden window, its white curtains curved by the evening breezes. Slowly my psyche would penetrate the night sky. Brightly shining stars seemed to call my name as visions of crystal bubbles floated softly above the horizon. Soon this silver space shattered all sense of reality. My intuition sensed *time* expanding beyond anything imagined. Infinite space unfolded, twisted and turned before my captured eyes. Spirals of energy seemed to release my repressed rage as whirling cyclones startled my psyche. Suddenly, openings appeared in space from which my mind might never return.

Such scenes shocked my senses. Changes began abruptly that strange Sunday morning when black clouds threatened the silver sky. The drawing room was charged with electricity! How Mother's mood reflected the brewing storm as she shifted silver objects from one antique table to another. Everyone became tense. Despite Father's refusal, Mother accepted an invitation for afternoon tea. Sunday papers remained unread. The fireplace left with dying embers, anxious and silent the

3

family drove down bleak country roads. My mind reeled from parental tensions. My tunnel eyes followed lightning streaks flashing across the sky, as my thoughts slipped beyond present time. The surrounding landscape disappeared as tall poplar trees became thick woodlands. Emerald green grass clasped hands with the silver sky, stretching to the river bank. Tall reeds graced the shore, and serene shadows floated upon still waters.

Suddenly scenes shimmered beneath overhanging branches, bizarre images unfolding within waves of glistening light. Then did strange visions appear before my *sight*. A meandering canal with a narrow boat named *Nebulae*, a curious Captain behind its rudder, silently guiding its bow through calm waters. A weathered lock before a lock keeper's cottage, red summer roses climbing its walls. When secure with these sights, my vision abruptly shifted. Why now my mind was within the surrounding woodlands! Warrior maidens were dancing by moonlight, and an ancient cave appeared. Then a peculiar crystal pond, snake reflections shimmering upon its waters. How my vision kept shifting between this frenzied forest and the calm canal. What had happened to my mind? Even the stone Manor house seemed a faraway apparition. Only when Father's black car stood before its ivy entrance did these scenes dissolve. Then did my head shake in shock. Having floated back from some deep trance, nothing around me seemed real.

That Sunday afternoon seemed forever. Desperately my body tried to remain in the drawing room, but my mind kept slipping away. Scenes of ritual rites and mirror ponds, a narrow boat and silver trident bombarded my psyche. Polite chatter of "tea and scones, raspberry jam and clotted cream" only made my anxiety mount. Restless from tension, some strange instinct pulled me towards the spiral staircase. Some strong intuition bade me to search its shadowed corridors of dark halls and crimson carpets. Faded family portraits watched me as I peered behind every open door. Had they snickered as I stood before the most bizarre of bedrooms? Had the smell of sulphur not pulled me towards its darkness?

Its green velvet curtains were half drawn. Did the shining sun, after the silver storm, not try to light its mysterious walls? Yet my eyes could hardly see the shadows of sensuous snakes wriggling through eternity. Serpentine shapes crawling up forest green walls to reach the crimson red ceiling. Endless tanks holding these creatures in captivity.

My thoughts turned to petrified stone. To whom could such a macabre bedroom belong? Who could have contained these eccentric creatures of the night? Geraint, the unapproachable one, came to mind. My intuition flashed "yes" as my imagination craved to know everything at once. What had inspired his outrageous passion? What dramas had unfolded in this bizarre bedroom? What secrets of his soul lay hidden here, and *why* had Geraint so carelessly left his bedroom door adrift?

Clearly a mirror of mystery shimmered within the mind of black haired, blue eyed Geraint. Yet he appeared so impersonal at school. Inflexible and detached, Geraint seemed more concerned with himself than schoolmates. His rebellious manner attracted caution and restraint. His remote ideas connected to the future. Never were his words in past or present tense. Did this strangeness not mirror the suspicion of snakes? Was his abruptness not the ability to strike at will, lest his plans be disturbed? Yet I, Aisling, had intruded upon his secret space. Such interference appealed to me. Yet surely it appalled Geraint, and his obsession became my quest.

How my mind bounced with bizarre thoughts, my curiosity craving to know everything at once. His strange passion for collecting snakes. The seclusion of serpents in his bedroom. The dialogue with his shadow self. The strategy of his suspicious snakes. My energy was ignited by eternity! Could Geraint be caught in a time warp? Come from another time and space frame? An alternate dimension, an outlying galaxy? Could his mind exist in multiple spaces at once? Then did such thoughts cease in shock. For had my words not described secret doubts I held about myself?

Geraint noted my return to the drawing room. Our eyes fastened on one another. Then did I watch him slide between conversations, brush past but never touch a guest. How my ears heard the hiss of his mind! High frequency vibrations pulsing with steady determination, my passion read his every thought. His secrecy pleased my sense of the surreal. His facade challenged my curiosity. How my mind tried to delve behind his mask of protection! Yet his smile listened without a spoken word. Only his studied silence suggested that strange events were coming. Yet, even without a sentence exchanged, his vibrations seemed intimate and ominous. Everything about Geraint felt familiar and fatal.

Unexpectedly, my energy started to spiral. Images rose of diamond snakes coiled around my arms, serpents laced within my satin hair. Visions of snakes falling as necklaces upon my bronze skin. Were these pictures not memories from some potent past? Something deep inside me knew these strange creatures who curled and curved, twisted and turned. Everything about this bizarre bedroom my eyes had seen before. Somewhere, sometime long ago, Geraint and Aisling had shared this strange fascination for exotic friends. How my obsession longed to know *when* and *where* and *why*!

My mind flooded with fantasy, visions filled with dramatic encounters in clandestine caves. Three females kept appearing before Geraint. First came the goddess Artemis with arched bow and silver arrows. Her virgin voice declared, "Pray speak of your encounters with the snake god Apollo!" The crescent moon shone above her forest hair. Woodlands surrounded her bathing nymphs. Then did mad Medusa come forth, her ravished hair now turned to serpent curls. The waning moon faintly glowed behind her ancient face, her scorching eyes petrifying men to stone. Wrathful Medusa furiously proclaimed, "Take care, for my *sight* knows the secrets of your soul!" Then did her shadow coil around his lean body, soft as a flute, tempting him with snake charms. Abruptly, the goddess Athena thrust her glistening shield within his trembling hands. "May the sun shine upon your days! May the wind carry you home! May heaven watch your ways!" were her fiery words. Yet only Artemis loved him as a brother. Mad Medusa wished to seduce his soul, while angry Athena commanded him to be the hero of her deeds.

Those vibrant visions framed as cameos, ancient sagas for my silent viewing. Myths from my eternal soul. Elusive and mysterious scenes. Shadows which kept Geraint alive in my mind were the opposite in reality. Here Geraint evaded my attentions. His physical self avoided my presence. Sparse school comments were strained. His black hair kept his blue eyes from me. His feet sought another direction. His cryptic smile refused my studied stares. Had my psyche angered his *sight*? Clearly my telepathic thoughts had displeased him, and my mental messages were not welcome.

Then did my fears turn frantic. How frustrated became my feelings! My voice yearned to shout that snakes were my passion. His serpents were physical, while mine were locked in the depths of dreams. Yet some strange chasm stood between us. What abyss held us apart? My impassioned mind delved into the past. Telescopic thoughts attempted to reach his ancient soul. How many evenings my psyche tried to explore centuries long gone! Yet no further visions came forth. Did the strength of his secrets shield his soul? Undaunted, determined to discover his hidden desires, my memory floated deeper into the depths of space.

My mind melted into the vast underworld of myths where my psyche reached serpentine fables. Magic mirrors swirling with nocturnal beasts, subterranean creatures meandering beneath these sensuous surfaces. Snakes with jewels beckoned me. Serpents sparkled with translucent red rubies upon their wisdom eyes. Snakes who pierced the facade of fate. Serpents of prophecy who mirrored the reflections of curves. Snakes who beguiled and bewildered. Creatures who swore to reveal their sacred lore to me, Aisling of the dream. How wondrous were these sensuous snakes! How I marvelled at their ways, always shedding and renewing their reptile skins. Bejewelled creatures poised between the sun and the moon, light and darkness, the sacred and the secret.

My dreams entwined with wriggling snakes! How visions surfaced of a Kingdom beneath the Sea guarded by a magical psychic Serpent Queen, an exotic world both familiar and fierce. Within these submerged depths swam the shadow of Geraint, a gold bird hovering above his head. Would dreams next disclose what memory had hidden in desires? Would *time* unfold secrets forgotten in space? Yet how much longer must I wait and wonder?

How my mind visualized Vivienne as the enticing mortal Queen who tempted Poseidon with her charms!

Suddenly, my world
turned in circles and
spun in spirals.

· II ·
THE
SILVER
BUBBLE

REJECTION MADE ME BURROW INTO BOOKS as my mind became my mentor. Suddenly, my world turned in circles and spun in spirals. For I, Aisling, began achieving in school, receiving recognition never known before. Pleasing teachers with my potential talent, hours spent in writing awakened my imagination. How my fingers flew! Blue ink pens wrote tales about galaxies united by trust, dimensions divided by doubt. Heroines who slipped through silver mirrors. Heroes who grasped the golden hands of time. Poems which unlocked secret passageways to space. Stories that dynamited the day, exploded nightmares of the night. My mind listened to my inner voices. How my thoughts raced, faster than fingers could write. Sagas appeared from pictures seen in dreams, sentences heard in my mind, intuition that moved fantasy into form.

School relaxed my frightened feelings, brought the challenge of change. Yet teenage years left me insecure and vulnerable. My rebellion needed to be *real*! The heroine yearning to greet the hero, longing for acceptance from another. Casual meetings were many, friendships few. My heart feared others might reject me, as Mother had many times before. Only when approached did I respond. Then did my mind remain suspicious, questioning while listening. Still, beneath my cool facade, how my heart yearned for a friend! Someone with whom secrets might be shared. Someone to whom my tales might be told.

How often I stood alone, without a soul in sight. My shattered psyche would listen to the chatter of classmates, to the nonsense they shared together. Then did I wonder *what* they were talking about. My eyes would watch the free and easy swagger of their walks. My heart would flutter: How does it feel to wear frivolous clothes? Be foolish with giggles? Flirt with boys? Murmur into someone's ear? Yet none of that seemed my way. I twisted my hair around my fingers, chose to be the last in line. Could awkwardness assure that no one would notice me?

Yet shyness was painful. Frightened feelings retreated before ever stepping forward. Only when alone did my anxiety relax, and my creativity explode. With the bedroom door securely shut, silence filled with fantasy. Evenings exploded into pages of poetry, tales of truth. My diary expanded, scribbled with sentences heard at school, daydreams of Geraint, rebellious plans to change my life. Yet something strange always interrupted me. Some curious feeling that drew me from the desk towards the breezeless window.

Hands tucked beneath my chin, I would straddle my red chintz chair, gaze into the garden. Evenings seemed eternal. My eyes would watch the sapphire sky unroll its magic carpet of flickering smiles. Clusters of stars, seen from a distance, glistened as glass. How my spirit stretched to dazzling dimensions! The blue velvet sky would rest upon my lap. Zodiac patterns appeared on my palms. Stars of silver brilliance sparkled as the serpent pathway in the sky. Always one crystal star beamed brighter than others. Mesmerized by its mystery, my mind would be drawn towards its shimmering light.

Night after night my eyes would watch this sight. How often silver sparkles became a brilliant pulsating beam! Then would all sense of *time* and *space* dissolve. My mind would merge with its magic. One bizarre evening its radiance became blinding, its blazing light transformed into a shining silver disk. In that strange second the Old Man of the Universe called, "the further you explore, the more sensitive are the vibrations you require." Yet my mind went blank. My concentration could not sustain the vision. Its magnetic energy became too intense. Everything began to blacken. Moved beyond memory, my psyche suspended in space, my mind had stretched beyond my thoughts. Then did my physical body succumb to a strange, intoxicating drowsiness. So it was that I drifted into an exhausted, almost drugged, sleep.

The pink satin dawn awakened me. Curled within the red chintz chair, my head felt heavy, fingers numb. Suddenly my startled eyes blinked in bewilderment. An eerie white glow silhouetted the lawn, an incandescent shadow casting a perfect circle upon the emerald grass. Had my mind fallen between shadow and light, craziness and sanity? Within this fierce illumination, a silver bubble now descended. Yet, between one breath and another, abruptly the vision vanished. The luminescent sphere evaporated into the stillness of night. Had my senses strained beyond reason? Had my mind gone mad? Had my astonished eyes truly *seen* a vision as fleeting as a dream?

At breakfast not a word was spoken. Had Father not noticed the circle of burnt grass upon the lawn? Had my brother not heard the noises of the night? Had my sister not been startled by the luminous light? "What's wrong with me?" "Am I completely crazed?" "Have I lost all my senses?" What mattered if my scrambled eggs turned cold? Who cared if marmalade toast stuck in my throat? All I wanted was to shout, "Why don't any of you *see* things?" My mind could hear everyone's exasperated words. "Aisling makes up tales." "Aisling needs to be tolerated." "Aisling is always imagining things." My psyche slithered away as a serpentine snake, and my emotions crawled beneath my skin. Thus did my *sight* become my secret held within.

Yet my mind vowed to unravel this riddle. Questions revealed only questions. Doubts followed doubts. Could my bedroom be a timeless void into the door of night? Was its open window beyond the walls of this world? Had my mind travelled further than the temptations of *time*? Was the silver bubble a shell of curved space? Yet no sign acknowledged these thoughts. The sky twinkled but did not dance. The garden grass remained without a scar. Silver stars seemed asleep. How many fretful nights did drowsiness become exhaustion. How my watchtower eyes would shut from fatigue. Still, evening after evening, nothing changed.

Tired of anticipation, my psyche surrendered. Suddenly the horizon appeared as a great upward curve. Serpentine stars turned into a spiral staircase. A silver metallic beam streaked across the black velvet sky. Within seconds, red and white blinking lights burst forth. A hidden world exploded with satellites and spaceships, meteors and messages from unknown realms. Yet this fantasy of fireworks lasted but a moment. Stillness followed silence. Determination to reach these realms surpassed all doubt.

My mind mastered the night sky. Soon my psyche could map the constellations, separate the Big Dipper from the Little Bear, shooting stars from planets. My dream compass soon clarified my thoughts. Only the Milky Way, the path of the serpent stood apart. Was this long ago memory not reminiscent of childhood dreams? Yet the Keeper of Time had never ventured to these serpentine stars. Was this the space he intimated I was to discover? How these millions of silver stars, formations of nebulae, seemed beyond time itself!

Then did I, Aisling, prepare to slip between these dimensions. How my mind sought spaces with the mystery of music. Suddenly, infinite choices seemed possible and probable. Perhaps silver stars might guide me through mystic places and timeless miracles. What if the Milky Way transformed into something else? Serpentine spirals which became a silver staircase. A shadow tunnel with luminous light at the end. A silver disk suspended in space. Sparkling crystal bubbles with windows to other worlds. Nothing could veer my mind from this force offering me other options. My breathing would near cease. My pulse became slow and shallow. How patiently did my psyche wait and watch!

Night after night nothing happened. Then, unexpectedly, one silver star might flash within the Milky Way. Its light would expand into a scooping funnel, and my mind would be drawn into its lightning sparks. Spiralling in a counterclockwise motion, its boundless beam swiftly spun into a silver disk. Then this strange shape would stand stationary in space. Electric lights would bounce from its shimmering surface. Ushered by whooshing sounds, a current of swift air pulled me into the vessel itself. Yet, once inside, the silver disk transformed into a flawless crystal bubble.

How this Silver Dream never left my sight! Soon worlds upon worlds unfolded before my eyes. Infinite space became endless eternity. Inside the crystal bubble were countless other bubbles, opaque within, silver without. Steering through serpentine stars, these floating spheres seemed soundless and effortless. A revolving crystal gyroscope energized and stabilized its every motion. An instrument guided by two transparent beings, androgynous mirror images. One clear crystal radiated the magic of *Ruby Red*, another beamed the mystery of *Diamond White*. Their heads glistened as crystal skulls. They conversed through telepathic thoughts, nothing stirred but their shining light! My spirit had returned home. This soundless language my psyche understood. Had my soul not spoken this way, many eons ago? Somewhere, some forgotten place, my mind had heard these conversations before. Somehow my thoughts could still hear faint echoes of:

Here, Aisling, voices are not heeded!
Here, Aisling, temptations are not touched!
Here, Aisling, wishes are not granted!

These crystal beings anticipated my every query. How they offered what was in my mind! Their one pointed concentration was profound, near dramatic. How the marvel of their magic remained a mystery! Diamond White mirrored my thoughts, helped my resistance to dissolve. Ruby Red flooded my mind with flames so fierce my hands shaded my eyes, while my vision became acclimated to their brilliant glow! Even my ears succumbed to a silence teeming with unseen things. Soon my body fathomed that all five senses were lost. Fingers and toes, hands and feet were without feeling. Touch was gone. Speech seemed senseless. Tastebuds no more. Perhaps this dimension belonged to dreams of destiny. Yet might my mind be tricking me again? Had my fantasy fallen into an endless sleep?

Always, as my eyes opened, these images dissolved abruptly. Nothing remained but memory. How my rational mind would study my seeming sanity. Suddenly my white organdy curtains were closed, the red chintz chair abandoned. My deepest desire hoped my dreams would explain this drama. Had Whisper not once said, "Have you ever watched yourself moving through your dreams?" Thus did my logic experiment with my seeming sanity. Resting on my back before sleeping, all senses relaxed into myself. With toes touching, hands crossed upon my stomach, my mind visualized me, Aisling, surrounded by a crystal egg, glowing white light from head to toe. Safe and secure in my four-poster bed, my breathing would deepen. All awareness of my physical body would cease. Lightness and warmth flowed through my veins. In this cocoon of calm, suspended in space, my body seemed to slip into a second sleep. Then would my dream self drift into the twilight zone. Hovering between waking and sleeping, I heeded Whisper's words! "Float, Aisling! Drift with your dream self! Fly! Fly! Fly!" So my dream self entered the shadow realm.

How my telepathic thoughts tried to contact Diamond White and Ruby Red! For three nights before sleep my body rested on its back, my mind floating freely. Three times the same request was repeated:

Please take me to the Silver Bubble!
Please take me to the Silver Bubble!
Please take me to the Silver Bubble!

Then my spirit waited in silence.

Only on the third night did a serpentine star flicker. Slowly my psyche melted into its pulsations. Without moving, my mind gazed upon its glow, with all feelings focused. A silver radiance filled the indigo screen of my dreams. Instantly did the night sky explode into dazzling light, transforming into a translucent silver sphere. This mysterious shape became a looking glass. Once within, the crystal ball mirrored other crystal bubbles. Yet now there were limitless smoky spheres, each projecting shadow images of myself. Smoky crystal screens which made my mind doubt my decision. For a dreaded moment the darkness consumed my sight. Then did my psyche cringe from projections of my past.

Abruptly my mind recalled the Wise Old Woman's words. "One who seeks the Light attracts the Dark. Creatures of blackness feed on fear, and the fear of doubt opens the darkest doors." Then did fleeting smoky crystals crash through my thoughts. They bombarded me from every direction! Frantically spinning through space, so each bubble near burst. My vision went berserk. Had my mind entered a multiple media of madness? Senseless smoky crystal spheres drifted in and out of space, revolved and swiftly spun. How my mind prayed for a crown of *seeing* eyes to encircle my head! Yet, when this wish was granted, what ensued? Why total chaos and confusion.

Visions of darkness appeared within twirling crystal bubbles, tormenting my *seeing* eyes! There were moods of despair and discontent. My fears floated before my face, my rage flaming in rays of Ruby Red as Diamond White mirrors reflected my deepest doubts. Smoky crystals returned my worried mind, recalled my yearning to escape. Whirling spheres demanded my attention. My face hidden behind my hands, my dream self could not leave. Some strange suction held me in place. Were my doubts to be witnessed until dissolved? Were dark thoughts calling to be cleansed?

Yet who had time to think such thoughts? My crown of *seeing* eyes spun faster and faster, whirling *out of control*. Smoky crystal bubbles now tilted and twirled, screamed at once, "Try me!" "How do you like that one?" "Who would trust her?" "There's no place to hide!" "How about another chance?" "What about this scene!" "There's nowhere to run!" Serpentine voices hissed, entwined around my ears. How my anguish shouted, "Stop! Stop! Stop!" Yet no one answered my plea.

Only then did my psyche surrender. My anger was accepted. My rage respected. Negative feeling forgiven. Slowly the dark crystal bubbles dissolved into flashing lights of red and white. Then did Ruby Red send blazing cardinal beams before my eyes. Crimson crystals flowed through my being. Fire red visions of serpents awakened my *sight*. Snake charmers praised my fortunes. Serpents with dazzling rubies in their mouths brought tokens of love. Then did Diamond White send shimmering bubbles of light to soothe my spirit. Crowning my head with a crescent moon, so the clarity of crystal entered my mind. Threads of silver stars streaked through my psyche. Then everything dissolved into dust.

My dream shattered into silent space. Were its vibrations too penetrating? Had not my mind lost touch with its visions? Suddenly my Silver Dream was gone. Only tremors of its telepathic thoughts remained. Faintly did words from the Old Man of the Universe reach me. "By not centering you lost both confidence and concentration. Even so, you saw much that can be drawn upon whenever needed." Yet had I, Aisling, not witnessed the marvel of a mirror? Never again would telepathic truths be denied. Had my mind not *seen* my negative thoughts destroyed? Had not my flames of fury been healed by Ruby Red, becalmed by Diamond White?

As I floated back into my physical body a strange voice spoke to my mind. "Aisling, Aisling, perhaps you have gazed within a crystal into which a serpentine star has fallen." Such a bizarre thought opened my eyes with a start.

"Aisling,
look to lands faraway,
for you are seeking stars once known."

· III ·

QUEEN
MEDUSA

SUDDENLY MY MIND FELT LIGHTER. Layers of depression had been shed from my skin. My heart wanted to fling aside the organdy curtains, open wide the windows, salute the sunshine day. My voice declared that demons of dread had dissolved. Twirling around the bedroom, my words proclaimed that Silver Dreams had changed my life.

My head began dancing with my heart! Was that truly Aisling who greeted the bus driver on the way to school? Was it really *me* whom Vivienne, with sea green eyes and red gold hair, sat beside? Were we actually chatting away? Classmates had turned their heads, wondering what was happening. Murmurs were heard. How it thrilled me to receive attention, though indirect. Yet, when the bus stopped at a red light, something inside me lost control. I made the mistake of speaking the unspeakable. Still, was there ever a *mistake*? Clearly my spirit had tired of nonsense talk. What strange sensation provoked me to ask Vivienne, "Do you dream at night?" Startled by this curious question she hesitated, then said, "No, the alarm wakes me up. My mind hardly remembers a dream." Then did my voice solemnly reply, "Neither does anyone in my family." After seconds of silence Vivienne stared at me. "Do you?" Was that the truth my heart wanted to tell? "Yes, my dreams come day and night. They always feel like going to the movies alone." Vivienne looked puzzled. Yet her sea green eyes were not as innocent as pretended. "What do you dream?" she slyly prompted. Should my voice speak of silver shadows and serpentine stars? Dare my words describe one Silver Dream and nothing more? Yet, as my excitement expanded, Vivienne squirmed. Her watery eyes and red gold hair poised on the edge of the cliff. Torn between safety and risk, my intuition hesitated. What if Vivienne just *looked* different, but was truly like everyone else?

Relieved when the bus arrived at school, Vivienne had smiled a quick smile

13

and hurriedly gathered her books. Her secure stare acknowledged our shared moments. Then something inside her snapped. "Have to dash!" she blurted. "Don't want to be late for class!" Her pace quickened as passing friends shouted, "Morning, Vivienne!" Suddenly my mind withdrew into my shadow. Yet speaking my truth made me feel lighter. Clearly my psyche craved contact with another, whether my dreams met with approval or not. During morning lectures positive *me* chose a front row seat. At lunchtime my tunnel eyes watched, but Vivienne did not appear. Perhaps her furtive Scorpio mood sought space. Yet my heart knew my secret was secure, we would speak again. Perhaps sooner than either thought.

The next time Vivienne sat beside me on the school bus, my confidence was shaken. Only after words were spoken did my anxiety relax. "Sorry for my rudeness last week," she awkwardly blurted, "but you scared me." Again, strange words sprang from my mouth. "It's all right," I replied. "But you curve like a snake." Vivienne, not surprised, smiled a knowing smile. Her clear green eyes showed fright. Something had turned them deep as sea water. Still her secret nature would not reveal what had happened. With hesitancy she finally confessed, "Aisling, you're really strange, and I like you." From that moment onward we were friends.

Whereas I was *strange*, Vivienne was *exotic*. Porcelain white skin against red gold hair, her entrance was always soft and seductive. She slid into rooms, and spoke slowly with cautious eyes and careful lips. "It's my Scorpio secret," she would say. Romantic books were read. Mysterious museums visited. How her fantasy lived in a visual world! Glistening jewels from the East, furniture inlaid with mother of pearl, silk embroidered cushions attracted her searching eyes. Her family drawing room, adorned with oriental carpets, tapestries of gold and silver threads, held carved statues in unexpected corners. On hot summer days vibrant umbrellas shaded the emerald green lawns. Life seen through Vivienne's eyes was Aladdin's magic lamp. Her reality was as opulent as my dreams. Our mutual imaginations overflowed with visions.

How she reminded me of every snake legend my psyche could recall. Yet my view of Vivienne vacillated between psychic Queen Medusa and mad Medusa whose ruby red eyes turned men to stone. How my mind imagined Vivienne as the enticing mortal Queen, tempting Poseidon with her charms. The audacious Queen who claimed her beauty equal to Athena, goddess of weaving and war. Still my psyche was perplexed by Vivienne. How often she seemed a serpent mystical and magical, with movements curving as a jewelled diamondback rattlesnake! Sometimes I pretended she was a wisdom snake, living in darkness, protecting unseen powers, secure in hidden secrets, her silent radiance guarding precious treasures of the mind. Other times Vivienne seemed another. Then was she seductive and sensual, theatrical and ancient, her portrait painted as potent, clever, cautious.

*How she belonged beside the ugly Gorgon Medusa! Were they not
mirror reflections seeking a balanced whole?*

Such thoughts became a fixation. Never could my mind imagine Vivienne without *seeing* snakes. Finally, my courage summoned, I confessed the unspeakable. Walking through school corridors, my voice shyly spoke. "Vivienne, may I tell you something?" Not surprised, she awaited my concern. "Why do you remind me of snakes? Why do I *see* you as psychic Queen Medusa, before Athena cursed her bewitching ways?" Vivienne suddenly stopped and smiled. "You mean intuitive Medusa with jewelled hair and impetuous eyes? Who partnered with Poseidon, lord of the waters? The god who seduced her in the Temple of Athena." Then did we relax, as our conversation became excited! How my words raced! "Vivienne," my voice exclaimed, "so you know the myth! That psychic Medusa was a mortal Queen. That her gorgon sisters flew with immortal golden wings." Vivienne interrupted, "That their hands were of brass. That huge tongues lolled from their mouths, dangling between tusks of swine. That their heads were entwined with snakes." Then did she hesitantly add, "Aisling, didn't you know they guarded the *sight* of mystery? So only they could *see* what was hidden to others."

We agreed that Queen Medusa was intuitive, impulsive, instinctual. That her passion was for creativity, not chaos. Yet her beauty so vain to believe herself equal to the warrior Athena. Was she not ready to be exposed by emotions? Why else would her impulsive spirit challenge the goddess of war? Vivienne imagined Queen Medusa as exotic, erratic, elusive. A bejewelled snake slithering through unknown realms. I, Aisling, visualized her moving through senses of sound, feeling by instinct. *Seeing* the mystery of each moment. Surely this myth was about the psychic sense, Queen Medusa using her intuition for emotions. While *sight* for the goddess Athena served as a web to be spun for war.

How strange that my dream that night brought the Old Man of the Universe. His distant voice called, "You are indeed a spirited soul to challenge such a one as I!" So had he chuckled in my sleep. Then the Keeper of Time guided me towards an ancient myth. "So you wish to know about psychic Medusa?" he had secretly smiled. "Then what of my three immortal sons? The ones who drew three lots. The gods who divided the power of the Universe amongst themselves." My eyes stared in astonishment. What had they to do with the *sight* of Medusa? Then did Whisper's childhood words resound clean and clear: "Aisling, look to lands faraway, for you are seeking stars once known." Suddenly my indigo dream shimmered with three crystal bubbles floating in space.

A dark revolving bubble held Hades, ruler of the Underworld. A golden crystal ball contained Zeus, sovereign of the Heavens. A turquoise crystal sphere spun with Poseidon, lord of Earth and Sea. Yet the sky shook with trouble and turmoil. Thunderous Zeus declared, "I, Father Heaven, am the highest and mightiest in the Universe!" Then from his head sprang the goddess Athena. Yet, having drawn the

15

second lot, did Poseidon jealously proclaim, "No, I am the first and forever!" How his crystal sphere trembled and quaked! He raged and swore revenge. "My tempers and temptations will never cease!" he cried. "May floods and tides quench the flames of mighty Zeus!" Then did Poseidon possess Queen Medusa in Athena's sacred temple. Thunderbolts flew across the sky. How Zeus raged! How Athena's wrathful voice cried out! "Poseidon, as no god may come to harm, so must mortal Queen Medusa bear this timeless curse! Her *sight* must be severed! Then your immortal offspring may come to birth!"

Abruptly did my Silver Dream transform again. Why, through the serene sky, flew my friend the Silver Bird! Gliding through metallic spaces, he was weaving musty webs of purple threads. Then did flutters of silver gauze stretch across wide waters. Clouds of swirling eddies melted caves of ice. Suddenly his sparkling silver wings flew into boundless space. From his distant shadow soared a crimson bird with golden wings. How its sun-bright luminescence dazzled my eyes! Yet, when the golden rays had vanished, winds thundered and tides rose high. Storms of silver snakes shimmered beneath silver waters, and behind each sensuous snake hovered serpentine shadows of Aisling and Geraint. Faintly did my dream self hear a mellow murmur. "Lifetime is Dreamtime. Dreamtime is Lifetime." No sooner were these words spoken, than the voice dissolved as dust.

What psychic vibrations were drawing us near? Crimson reds and sapphire blues were flashing before my eyes. Geraint was mesmerized by a sapphire and ruby bird flying to Heaven, while a magic gold sword pierced my *sight*. Then I, Aisling, was astride a white winged horse, sparkling diamonds falling from my mouth. What had happened? Suddenly my dream self was wearing a gown of white. My long hair glistened with silver stars. The crescent moon shone above my head. My body silent, a strange voice within me slowly spoke of things to come. What hidden secrets had my Silver Dream brought to light?

That very next morning how the bathroom mirror startled me! While brushing my hair, my eyes blinked in shock. Before my frightened face the ancient myth loomed strong. The reflection in the mirror was not mine, but gallant Geraint. A golden helmet, adorned with a wolf, was upon his head. His strong hands held a gold sword. Then did he vanish and Vivienne appear. Yet the mystical Queen Medusa was now a hideous hag with hair of snakes. Beauty had become the beast, and I, Aisling, was astride the white winged horse. What bizarre connections were bringing us all together? What frightening forces had been unleashed? What powerful vibrations were pulling at our lives?

That night I frantically began to write. Sentences flowed from angry Athena, words of wrath from the warrior goddess, betrayed in her sacred temple. Was it because she reminded me of Mother, somehow dishonored in her own home? How my

16

mind resounded with the fury of her cries!

How dare Poseidon and Medusa abuse my sacred Temple! She who rivals my beauty, and a mortal Gorgon Queen as well! May her jewels never allure a god again. May her eyes petrify men to stone. May her ravishing hair turn to writhing snakes, her tongue to silence, her eyes the blood of ruby red. May men cringe from the sight of her horror, die from a look at her face.

Then, with haste, did my pen write about Perseus, the hero who slew Medusa.

You mortal brother of Athena, son of Zeus, brother of Apollo! Why did you take Athena's shining shield to sever mad Medusa's head? Never did you gaze into her psychic eyes. Instead you slew her reflection in the mirror. And what of the two drops of blood upon the ground? Did you not birth the offspring of mortal Queen Medusa and Poseidon? Pegasus, the mysterious white winged horse of creativity. The magic gold sword of Chrysaor which cut through all illusion. Yet mad Medusa was potent, dead or alive. Did you not keep her bloody head within your pouch, taking it out to turn your enemies to stone? Did Athena later not place it upon her shining shield? Yet *why* were you so willing to sacrifice the Gorgon Queen? *What* strange passions drove you forth?

Suddenly did all writing cease. My mind was mesmerized by these words. What mysteries lay hidden behind the mask of this myth? Then did I, Aisling, pledge myself to mad Medusa, to gaze into her mirror and survive. My psyche vowed to unravel the reflection of this hideous hag and mystical Gorgon Queen! Something strong demanded that her psychic powers return to rule, that puzzling Queen Medusa, pregnant with clarity and creativity, be rebirthed without a murderous act. The stone of death would become the brilliant jewel of life again.

Surely serpents, ancient and ageless, were binding us all together. Had Geraint not appeared with snakes visible and potent? Observing them in glass tanks before forest green walls? Cool and controlled, his studied silence aware that serpents were dangerous and deceitful. That their poison demanded sacrifice, brought instant death. And Vivienne, with psychic eyes so like a snake. Did her Scorpio stare not keep others in suspense? Elusive and evasive, abruptly did her serpentine coils appear, then quickly disappear, her erratic energy held by high tension. A snake wis-

17

dom offering gifts of precious pearls, glistening jewels, sliding on the tightrope of risk.

Yet Vivienne's serpentine curves intrigued me. How she illuminated mystery, enchantment, magic! The intensity of a silver moon. While gallant Geraint disturbed my mind. Radiating heat from fiery flames, his shadow blazed with fierce rays of the sun. Clearly between their contrary ways a cryptic message coursed. How well my mind could hear distant Geraint. A ponderous thought to move my psyche past the present.

"He recovered his *sight* when a grateful serpent laid a precious stone upon his eyes."

Then, for the first time, did my mind accept a communication without challenging its meaning.

*"Just call me
Captain Nodi.
Captain Nodi will be fine."*

· IV ·
NARROW
BOAT
NEBULAE

AISLING, STOP DAYDREAMING. COME TO DINNER! How often had Father's voice resounded through the house. "Aisling daydreams too much." So my report cards read from school. "Aisling still gazes out the drawing room window," my piano teacher complained. Yet none had recognized my psychic shift, or noticed that my mind was sketching stories later to be written. No one seemed to see me reading serpentine fables before the fire in Father's library. Instead, they only observed that silence filled my days.

Yet what strange worlds now saturated my psyche. Sentences poised with infinite queries. Questions held an urgency for answers. My impatience craved knowledge at once. No longer the pride of my parents, other things mattered to my mind. I wondered if Geraint knew the ancient lore of snakes, or that the goddess Artemis had been a priestess, *the huntress one must hunt*. That her brother, the god Apollo, had killed the Great Serpent Python, protector of priestesses and oracles from Mount Parnassus. That his priests had replaced the female goddess with a male divinity. How they had used oracles for potency and power. How they had changed the laws of the land. Surely Vivienne knew that snakes brought death and destruction, wisdom and wealth. That their powers healed what needed to be restored. That their skin shed itself and regenerated anew.

How often my serpentine thoughts replayed these sacred myths. When the silver bell announced dinner, my mind would be somewhere else. Perhaps musing about Artemis the huntress, goddess of the virgin moon, birth of wondrous things to come. Perhaps imagining Geraint as sun god of snakes, wearing the mask of Apollo, his powers restoring the female oracle to her shrine. Maybe visualizing Vivienne saving mad Medusa whose hair had transformed to snakes. Even thinking of Mother as angry Athena, now weaving peace instead of war. Yet always I, Aisling, was seen as a prophetess with *sight*.

How often my tunnel eyes stared out school windows. In such stillness did questions spiral, only to entangle with many webs, as on and on the threads unraveled. Who was elusive Medusa? Was she a psychic mortal Queen? A triple goddess with her gorgon sisters? A temptress with snake charms? A female sorceress with *sight*? Had she provoked or permitted Poseidon, god of waters, to embrace her in the sacred temple of Athena? Why, from her severed head, had fallen two drops of blood, two magical beings? Who were these figures in this mysterious myth? Endless questions needed answers. Yet beneath the surface lay a sacred structure. Why had snake lore been shrouded in secrets? Why had masks concealed its mysteries? Why had ancient dramas deceived, kept believers from the truth?

Such visions required solitude, a readiness to receive. Yet a strong sense of not belonging always followed such seclusion. Being out of time brought longing to my life. The more muddled my thoughts, the more my mind needed clarity. How I wanted to know *what* realms such myths reflected. How I wondered *why* day visions differed from night dreams! Surely times awake connected to hours asleep. Yet my curiosity could not cope with interference from others. How the rational minds of parents and peers did rage! How their suspicions would scold. "Fantasy fills your days. The real world is where you should be. Imagination will never change your life." Such reprimands always caused depression. Then I would surrender to the present, yet clock time proved impossible. How my thoughts would wander, slip into other spaces and places. How my mind would mesh past, present, future all together!

Only daydreams had seemed different. Then had my private world filled with thoughts of escape. Imaginary scenes kept me safe from the hostility of home, the seclusion of school. My mind would blank out when anxious, stay alert when feeling fine. Yet daydreams were never spontaneous. Their images were guided by conscious thoughts. Scenes changed with whims of fantasy. Pretend pictures bolstered fragile feelings. Daydreams were treasures of wishful thinking, idyllic sagas that dissolved. Make-believe emotions which evaporated as night blanketed the day. Memories lingered but nothing else. Only hopeful feelings kept them alive. How they were an avoidance of something unpleasant. How they distanced me from demands. Yet they seemed a sleeping wakefulness, an illusion better than life.

Silver Dreams shifted these sensations. Suddenly my concentration increased. My mind and body stayed in the same place. I stopped thinking of Geraint while combing my hair. My psyche stopped slipping into stars while studying for school, and all faculties focused on events before me. My emotions accepted the atmosphere of home. No longer did I attempt to change the unchangeable. My mind stayed alert when Mother raged. No longer did I wonder *what* Father was doing away from home. My attention became acute. Something had shifted. "You have gone through a crack in the sky and, although it feels like a dream, it is not." Such words from the Wise Old Woman comforted my changing psyche.

In deep states of relaxation, my writing became spontaneous. Thoughts flowed from my mind. Intensity erased everything but pen and paper. Hours elapsed without notice. Slowly did my writing become a discipline. Afternoon light would turn to dusk, glistening stars would cover my bedroom with velvet peace. Serenity surrounded my psyche. An elusive essence pervaded the atmosphere. My right hand would poise in anticipation. Watchful eyes witnessed sentences unfold. How my mind would slip to the canal hidden by tall meadow grass. Strange thoughts described scenes never *seen* before. My eyes would read these curious words again and again. Then did I wonder, could such a vision come true? A Silver Dream that might later become a reality?

Once upon a time, long ago and maybe even now, there flowed an ancient canal which drifted past pastoral lands, under blackened tunnels hidden beneath arched footways. Through moonlit nights and morning mists its shimmering waters guided a mysterious narrow boat. Black canvas covered its working hull. Deep blue was the color of its trim. Painted with red roses and romantic castles, its outside was not unlike other narrow boats. But inside it was magic.

Shining brass lanterns lit its intimate cabins. Mugs, steaming with freshly brewed coffee, rested near a coal burning stove. Hot soup wafted cooking smells to the deck above. Smoke hooted through its blackened chimney. Soft hums from the brass engine glided the narrow boat beneath overhanging branches, near white lily pads, before iridescent ducks. Plates laced with shiny satin ribbons, strung along burnished oak walls, clanked and clattered as the boat meandered. Yet not a plate was ever chipped.

Seventy-two feet long and seven feet wide was what this boat named Nebulae claimed with pride. Here what was stuck as molasses soon flowed as honey. Yet none spoke too quickly nor disappeared from sight. Here the unexpected brought about the least expected. Visions of the night replaced scenes of the day. Those who visited were many, those who remained were few. Having come through waters of change, clearly certain persons had been called.

21

Once it happened, long ago and maybe even now, that a young maiden
was enticed to come aboard ...

Suddenly my writing ceased. No further words flowed from my pen. Yet
what if these sentences described a scene that came to be? Half of me hesitated, the
other half was intrigued. Then did my mind conceive a plan. Impulsive fingers scribbled hasty notes. Father would find them on the breakfast table. How Mother wondered what they were about. "Gone for a walk, back soon. Love, Aisling," was all
the words would say. Then did my feet trample through neighboring meadows. How
my senses explored the river bank as my tunnel eyes searched the calm canal. My
ears listened for engine hums upon its waters.

How many boats drifted by! Some with red geraniums and white narcissus,
others with bicycles for gathering goods. Yet no narrow boat called Nebulae cruised
the canal as my eyes read every name outlined in black. "Trident," "Jasmine," "Water
Lily," "Bluebell," "Rose of Heaven." Canal boats that once had carried coals to New-
castle. My eyes became accustomed to roses and castles, romantic scenes brightly
painted in reds, yellows, blues, and greens. Harlequin cards of hearts and diamonds,
aces and spades. Symbols of dreams and drifters. Travellers who lived apart from the
tensions of time.

Soon my doubt decided this was but another illusion. Perhaps my writing described something long ago. A remembrance of some forgotten memory. Still this
water way of life, calm and creative, appealed to my senses. Soothed by river
breezes, my mind drifted light and free. Hidden by tall grass, my feet dangled in cool
waters. Often not a dog barked, not a narrow boat meandered by, not a person passed
the tow path. In this undisturbed silence my thoughts flowed as smoothly as water.
All senses seemed relaxed, alive, receptive.

Unforeseen, arising from this reverie, a distant narrow boat attracted my attention. Coming through the weathered locks, its black canvas was unfurled, its
trim of deep blue. Then did my eyes see its curious Captain, with curly silver hair
and a stained white cap. He looked an ancient soul whose steadfastness could steer
the moon across the sky. Did he not steer the narrow boat as one driving a golden
chariot of the gods? How his turquoise eyes controlled the current of the waters. He
seemed so self-righteous and stern! "Perhaps a sea green mermaid should be tattooed
upon his arm." Yet what if he heard my teasing thought? Instead, the surly man
watched my studied stares. Then did an intuitive smile, a sensitive hand, and
twinkling eyes invite me to come aboard.

Drawn by the riddle of my writing I ventured forth. And what awaited me?
Why, once inside the narrow boat, everything seemed enchanted. Viewed through a

"He belongs to no realm, yet exists everywhere at once,"
Captain Nodi calmly said.

veil of white light, my feet stepped into another world where all was peaceful, contained, radiant, and relaxed. Yet, to my astonishment, the Captain had a keen thirst for possessions. Hanging on oak walls were plates strung with green satin ribbons. Scenes of white horses, golden chariots, coral conch shells, storms, and streams covered their porcelain surfaces. In the distant corner, above the blackened stove, copper pots and pans glistened. Suddenly did my eyes stop and stare. A strange silver trident sparkled near the cabin steps. The Captain, however, took no notice. He grinned a satisfied smile, spoke not a word. Then did my voice timidly ask, "What's your name?" His twinkling turquoise eyes pretended to ponder. "Nodiesop," he said. "Just call me Captain Nodi. Captain Nodi will be fine." There seemed a million meanings behind his name, a thousand thoughts behind his smile. Infinite spirals swirled through my mind. What made him seem so ageless and wise, measured and mean? Powerful was his presence, yet some instinct warned that Captain Nodi might be infamous. Yet, slippery or not, my psyche persevered. Nothing feared his forceful manner. Aware that his moods might turn me upside down and toss me inside out, still my sense of self decided to venture forth.

Had Captain Nodi heard these unspoken thoughts? Abruptly his eyes penetrated my gaze. Then slowly did he smile and say, "Would you care to see the rest of the narrow boat Nebulae?" My heart leaped with excitement! Then Captain Nodi showed me every detail. There were brass gas lamps that swayed with the river current. Covered bunks that became sleeping beds. A blackened coal stove whose fires needed tending, and a copper teapot that whistled like a bird. Above board were ten-foot poles to push the narrow boat from muddy shores. Mops, striped in red and white, for swabbing the upper deck. There were red geraniums and blue narcissus waiting to be watered, brass portholes needing to be polished, and a smoky chimney stack that had never been cleaned. Below deck, near the silver trident, swung a cage of brass which held the most fantastic bird my eyes had ever beheld. An outlandish creature, neither rainbow parrot nor white wisdom owl, neither falcon nor fierce hawk. It seemed an exotic combination of every bird, but more. Sapphire blue wings spread full across the cage. An electric blue face beamed with jet black eyes. Yet, coming from feathers of crimson red, blazed a powerful golden beam. My body stepped backwards. Had my mind *seen* clearly? Had the penetrating glare of this bizarre bird not been filled with fiery flames?

"He belongs to no realm, yet exists everywhere at once," Captain Nodi calmly said. Then did he watch my every reaction, measure my every movement. Without further comment he added, "His name is Adurag. Just call him Urag. Urag will be fine." Captain Nodi then offered hot lemon tea. Slowly he began a tale about a secret Kingdom under the Sea. Staring into my waiting eyes, he started his strange story.

Once upon a time a maiden sought a wondrous world where she might settle. Somewhere, long ago, she had heard murmurs of a mysterious realm seething far below the sea. A precious Kingdom under the depths of emerald green waters. Tales were told that within this jewelled sea lived the Serpent Queen of all life. It was said that her sacred Kingdom nourished female wisdom. That its forbidden lands contained curious creatures and crystal palaces filled with silver treasures and secrets of the soul.

To search for this strange place the seeker had to discard all normal ways. Only exceptional, divine beings survived in this Kingdom below the Sea.

Dangerous were its depths to probe. Endless taboos existed between the elusive sea and the lonely traveller. Few ever found the marvelous universe of this lost paradise.

Yet one dark night, when the silver moon was strong, a maiden dreamt a deep dream about water folk at sleep.

Amidst whirlpools winding in spiral motion, the maiden beheld a being with skin of bluish hue, hair with tint of green, legs turned to fishtail. As the whirlpools spun with waves, so this creature of immortal blood reached an opening within a darkened cave. Here waters overflowed into a still pool which acted as a mirror. As the maiden breathed upon its surface, so the pond cleared. Then did she *see* within its waters exotic images of things that were, things that are, things that yet may be.

Surrounding this still pond, hidden by trees overgrown with creeping ivy, stood a patch of grassy quiet. Yet none of this reflected on its surface. Beneath the waters could be seen only a narrow winding causeway of living rocks. Those aware of this path found their way through the pool into a citadel surrounded by glowing candles.

Waves of exquisite perfume, fifty feet deep but hardly navigable, spun themselves around the castle. Here fountains spouted wines scented with the aroma of cinnamon. Large crystal rooms were heated with tubs containing liquid honey and hot dew.

Through a door of ivory and ebony, one brave enough to enter came upon a passage paved with marble. Festooned with embroidered curtains of serpentine snakes, the passageway led to a further tunnel below. Here was a polished marble floor with pearls of running water. These waters, cold in the hottest of summers, never froze in winter.

In this faraway paradise ...

Suddenly Urag began cawing with high shrieking sounds, and Captain Nodi ceased speaking. The bird's shrillness had shattered the surrounding peace. Pressing his crimson face against the cage of brass, Captain Nodi spoke words I dared not hear. Flapping his sapphire wings, Urag demanded something beyond my understanding. When Captain Nodi disagreed, the brass cage dissolved into air. My mouth opened, did not close. Had my eyes not *seen* this bizarre bird stretch its wings wider than the boat itself? Had my mind not beheld his sapphire wings become radiant gold light? Had my ears not heard his screeching sounds turn to melodious song? Captain Nodi waited while I gasped. Then did the brass cage reappear, empty. Without a word, Captain Nodi brewed fresh lemon tea. Not heeding my confusion, he continued his tale of the Kingdom below the Sea.

In this faraway paradise the feminine spirit guarded the flowing waters. Here the Serpent Queen ruled as a king. A mistress of riches difficult to reach, dangerous to find. The treasures of this Kingdom were found below the bottom of the sea itself. In the depths of this emerald sea it was always night. Hell was everything that was hidden.

The Serpent Queen dreamt her life. Whatever happened was a silver mirror of her thoughts. When she threw a ball of silver thread at an invisible glass boat, the Serpent Queen would reel in this magic thread. What she brought to herself was always a faithful reflection of her innermost beliefs.

Now one unexpected night this mystical Serpent Queen...

Suddenly, only snoring could be heard. Captain Nodi had lulled himself to sleep. How I waited, yet he stirred not. Sadly, my feet tiptoed from the narrow boat Nebulae, as my heart made a wish beyond all wishes. How I hoped that the baffling Captain Nodi would greet me again at the river's edge. My psyche wanted to believe that this strange scene was not a dream within a dream but rather reality itself!

25

Then, with the eyes of a wolf,
young Geraint would see
into the dark unknown.

· V ·

SNAKE
SECRETS

SUNDAY MORNING. The air outside was cool and crisp. The sun slowly rising above the horizon. All windows were tightly shut, velvet curtains drawn, the still air stagnant from breathless hours. Within these deep green walls nothing disturbed Geraint. Untidy from restless sleep, a blue bathrobe hung loosely on his frame. His yellow pajamas, crumpled as unchanged bed linens, went unnoticed. Brown suede slippers, frayed at the edges, hardly held his feet. His pallid face completed this portrait of a crazed scientist or raving poet. Tense with excitement, Geraint's magnetic eyes peered into the *third eye* of a diamondback rattlesnake. Geraint sensed the coming of a breakthrough, his trembling mind aware that the poisonous serpent could strike at will.

Since 4:00 A.M. he had been concentrating on this prize rattlesnake, his gaze confident of alluring whatever it wished. Geraint's blue eyes were luminous, an electric-magnetic stillness surrounding his psyche. Measured thoughts had been conversing through even breaths. Mind to mind, soul to soul. How many questions had Geraint asked? How many answers had been received? Was his dream, to communicate with a venomous snake, about to be realized? To control the forces of nature, and tame psychic energy through the power of his mind. Clearly his soul connected to mysterious forces beyond the minutes of time. Surely his potency came from behind the veil of silence.

Born before the sun was upon him, Geraint sensed the psychic strength of the night. Twelve days after his last birth date he had begun to collect snakes. Carefully had he chosen from 2,000 species. Now, near the twelfth night of this soon to be completed year, he vowed to honor their serpent power. Why then did childhood nightmares loom before him? Unexpectedly he remembered the ways of the wolves. He *saw* these creatures of valour and evil, but no longer were they protecting his

27

soul. Their power was not shielding him from the fiery rays of the sun. In that instant the forces of Heaven entered his eyes and the influence of night ceased. The day ordered him to obey its command. Then did the strength of the sun summon Geraint to slay the psychic female Python. Its scorching rays melted the serpent's mystical form. Unforeseen, the oracle became his to protect.

Now, at this birth date celebration, Geraint suddenly felt caught between the struggle of sun and moon, day and night, life and death. Why had the memory of his Grandfather suddenly become alive? Geraint could almost *see* the worn tartan blanket across his Grandfather's knees. The hearth fire burning brightly, the dogs barking, the upstairs floors creaking, and the teakettle whistling from afar. How his young self had watched Grandfather savour his pipe, sip his tea. Grandfather's absent eyes would look away, then towards Geraint, his Celtic words spoken slowly, "Aye, boy, you were born in the darkness before sunrise, with eyes that came from wolf-light, from a darkness only wolves can *see*." How the fiery embers would crackle, the sitting room suddenly chill! Dusk of day would envelop the room. Grandfather, bending near, would whisper, "Aye, son, the wolves are coming soon!" Then, with the eyes of a wolf, young Geraint would *see* into the dark unknown, the forest of his mind safe from harm.

How demons would haunt his sleep! Frightful dreams of the flaming sun filled this Celtic memory. Nightmares screaming the legitimacy of his birth would be tested. Deadly serpents would surround him for twelve days and twelve nights. If no harm came then, indeed, Geraint was of pure birth. Thus had twelve become his potent number. Each year, precisely within twelve days and twelve nights, had he given birth to something extraordinary.

Yet the hours of bewitching were coming to a close. Secrets held within his head began to burst. Then did he recall Grandfather telling tales the bards had sung. How his grey beard had been soft to touch, his teeth stained from age. Snug before the glowing fire, young Geraint repeatedly heard the same sacred stories of snakes. "Son, do you know the serpent origin of Kings?" Grandfather would ask, then purposely pause. "Aye, snakes guarded their treasures and wealth. A visiting serpent was a sign of recognition!" To which excited young Geraint would add, "Grandpa, I have *seen* them in my dreams. Snakes with jewelled necklaces and gold crowns. Serpents speaking to me!" Thus tempted, Grandfather would slowly continue, "Once upon a time a king of wealth died without an heir. At night his soul returned in the form of a snake to guard his riches. This serpent spirit visited mountains filled with gold, where splendid snakes waited in the dark. Adorned with turquoise, emeralds, and coral, they told of submarine palaces filled with treasures of precious stones, and memories of secret teachings."

Yet that was all Geraint could remember. Now, with eyes of a wolf, he pre-

28

pared to leap into the dark unknown. Was the eleventh hour of the twelfth night not nearing? Was this not the time to proclaim his vow for the coming year? Only one anonymous oath had he avoided. A pledge which would push him into the abyss. Secretly Geraint had avoided sacred sites, shrines where serpents once delivered their oracles, where snake deities had imparted divine messages to a priestess of perfect purity. How Geraint feared sites sacred to the moon! Intuition made him anxious. The knowledge of things unseen brought tension. Yet he needed to master these insights to control whatever flowed through his mind. He knew the female python once protected these sites. Had she not been the guardian of each priestess? Childhood nightmares had shown Geraint slaying this psychic python. Each morning his body would quake with fear, and in terror would he vow to return this fallen female serpent to its rightful place of honor.

Slowly did Geraint welcome snakes into his secret chambers. His bedroom received them as agreeable guests, if not guardian spirits. Snakes were honored as his household gods. How their spirits intertwined. Yet, in strange ways, Geraint became dependent upon the safety of his snakes. Untouched food meant his protectors would forsake him. Jars of honey were kept to appease them in times of trouble. How he watched what they ate, what they discarded. To harm such dwellers was a deadly sin. Grateful serpents brought mysterious gifts to their benefactor. Desirous of such rewards, Geraint attended his guests with great care.

Believing himself destined to be a hero, unforeseen forces directed his mind. Thus for twelve days and twelve nights had he watched the movements and reactions of these very snakes. How many hours had Geraint stared into the *third eye* of his deadly diamondback rattlesnake? His psyche had obeyed each twist and turn of the potent snake. Carefully did he interpret each sacred sign. Should his snakes forsake him, danger or death was coming. Yet, should these deadly creatures coil through his arms, wrap around his waist, life was safe and secure. To appease his snakes Geraint played the flute. The music of the gods brought joy, love, and sweet sleep. Melodious sounds relaxed his revered rattlesnakes, that they might impart gifts of prophecy.

Through telepathic thought Geraint aspired to receive future solutions to present problems. Warnings of danger, death, and destruction, could magnify his power. Should disaster strike, Geraint could forecast its outcome. Yet to heal negative energy was his deepest desire, so he had chosen the deadliest, mightiest diamondback rattlesnake as his teacher. Since childhood had he vowed never to kill for vengeance, punishment, or revenge. This lifetime would be one of atonement. Thus had he pledged himself to tame the untamable, communicate with forces unknown.

Yet Geraint remembered warnings from the customs of the Celts. How his Grandfather had cautioned him! "Since long ago have people feared dangerous and destructive serpents. Geraint, become immune to their bites! Then may you attain power over their psyche." Thus had Geraint collected three venomous snakes known to be harmless—the king snake, water snake, bull snake. Then he obtained six poisonous snakes who could kill at will. The Arizona coral snake, water moccasin, Texas rattlesnake, copperhead, European viper, and the diamondback rattlesnake. Carefully had he chosen the latter as his master.

For twelve months had Geraint learned the habits of this capricious creature. Without limbs, eyelids, or external ears, he watched it move in series of waves. He had *seen* its sense of smell fuse with the caution of clarity.

Its pointed teeth appeared as a forked slender tongue, holding its body in suspension. Without vocal cords, the poisonous diamondback rattlesnake could hiss with a special sound-producing apparatus. How often did it strike a victim with lightning speed? Its power for destruction never left Geraint's conscious mind. This dark side hovered as a deadly omen. Always did such anger bring death.

Yet such snakes also symbolized immortality. How they shed one skin, only to grow another again and again! Hidden in subterranean regions, secretive snakes sought dark holes through cracks in earth and rocks. How often Grandfather had murmured, "Aye Geraint, a hero who seeks immortality must venture to the underworld. There must he seek the City of Serpents." Then had young Geraint's magnetic blue eyes widened. Soon Grandfather would speak of daylight and dreams, life and death. "Do you know, son," he would slowly say, "The web of night and day is stitched with black and white threads. Bound together with the red thread of life." How young Geraint would shudder! Then would Grandfather tie the knot of terror. "Aye, she who gave *sight* to the dead was called the mystical Queen of Serpents." Pausing for a moment he would add, "Aye, son, the gate of dreams and portal of death are one and the same."

Then did the present connect with the past. Had ancient oracles not been delivered by females before the light of the moon? Might they connect to the mystical Queen of Serpents? In that bizarre moment dawn broke through the night. How Geraint thought he heard the cries of a wolf. Then did Grandfather's voice ring through the room, speaking in present time. In whispered tones he said, "Aye, the Serpent Goddess embraced the king every night. Should the psychic queen not appear, this meant the king must be killed and a new king chosen." His voice rang from afar as Geraint held his breath, "Her serpents were purple with divine essence. Her people snake-like with forked tongues, great wisdom, and longevity." Now no part of Geraint stirred. "From the heart of the mysterious Serpent Goddess came mystical mermaids who received souls of the dead. Yet her womb was Paradise. Those ordained entered this dark tunnel of death and dreams to receive immortal wisdom."

Was it any wonder that Geraint feared the female power of a priestess? With clarity of crystal did he comprehend his task. Feminine energy belonged to the

H<sub>ow many hours had Geraint stared into the third eye of his
deadly diamond back rattlesnake?</sub>

sensuous snake. Only after he had slain the mystical python did their psychic power perish. Then had priests taken the title of serpent. Had they not been called "the ones who charm the snake"? Surely what had been divine became dominated by desire. How Geraint had breathed deeply, accepted surrender. With sudden awareness, on this twelfth night of all nights, was he ordained. Solemnly did he dedicate his oracle to female laws of the land. Thus Geraint promised to defend harmony of sea and sky. Somber, he stood before the diamondback rattlesnake, vowing his honor as a hero.

> "Through prophecies shall my soul give mortals reliable advice.
> "Through divination shall my spirit be healed and all those who come before me."

Then Geraint paused for an auspicious moment and bowed his head.

> "Through revelation shall the female oracle be restored to her rightful place of honor."

As the sun peered through the dark velvet curtains, Geraint pondered. Who might be Pythia, the goddess who once had served the awesome female python? His mind instantly flashed to Aisling! Yet Geraint cringed from the memory of that fatal Sunday afternoon. How it still haunted him! Why had his bedroom door been left open? Never had he been so careless. Such negligence could have harmed his snakes. His concerned eyes had noticed Aisling absent from tea. No doubt her curiosity had been satiated. Suspecting his secret discovered, Geraint kept distance between them. Yet what desire had drawn her away from tea and scones? Surely there were no accidents, only energy attracting attention.

As morning arrived Geraint heard the whistling and turnings of a violent wind. Strange sounds resembled the hissing of a rising snake, slipping through window panes behind his closed velvet curtains. Cautiously did he part the dark green fabric to permit the morning light. Then a strange sentence pierced his tired mind.

> "I *see* only darkness lying before her. Darkness and the shadow of another's fate."

Abruptly an image of a mermaid swimming through clear waters flashed before his startled eyes. A mystical female, human and serpent, drinking from the waters of a spring. Seated on a raised tripod, slowly this maiden inhaled fumes arising from burning essence. Geraint shook his head in shock. In this instant of amazement, everything dissolved from sight. How his hands trembled! Had he penetrated a moment beyond time itself? Panicked, once again did he renew his vow. "Yes, yes! My pledge shall be fulfilled this very next year. The female oracle shall be freed! The *sight* of the psyche shall be honored again!"

Yet whom was he reassuring?

How these woodlands thrived
from some strong female energy.

· VI ·
WOODLANDS AND WATER

HOW THE SILVER DREAM HAUNTED ME. Smoky crystal screens had shifted my psyche into another space. No longer did I, Aisling, seem the same person. Clearly the crystal bubble had untangled my negative web of thoughts. Had the Silver Dream not brought dynamic energy back into my life? Decisions now followed thoughts, feelings reacted to my surroundings. Suddenly there seemed no coincidences, only mirror reflections. Had night visions not unraveled my emotions? Had each dream message not been *me* in the process of change? Had the switch happened because I, Aisling, could neither control nor manipulate these images? No doubt the Silver Dream transformed me during the night. Upon awakening my psyche had shifted, and only then did other possibilities present themselves.

Had the Silver Dream released ancient memories from times past? Powerful images now guided my spirit to spaces behind guarded gates. Secure in my feelings, my spirit ventured deeper and further. Yet the Silver Dream had shifted my energy from the world of dreams to the world of reality. How my curiosity craved to know, "Which came first? The dream or reality?" Suddenly it did not matter. My mind seemed to link everything together. Each experience unfolded from the other, there was no separation. One event mirrored another. No longer need my dreams question reality, no longer need reality doubt my dreams. Were dreams not the world of unconscious images? Reality the conscious world of choice? Clearly one could not exist without the other.

Free from negative thoughts, how fantasy filled my day. How my body followed my head and heart. Suddenly I, Aisling, became an adventuress. Rather than meander through meadows towards the river, my feet turned in the opposite direction. Where did my intuition take me? Why towards the woodlands, away from Captain Nodi and the canal. Some strange instinct led me to sunlight shimmering

33

through overhanging branches. Lacy leaf patterns danced on tangled brambles. Cypresses and pines enclosed a silence alive and trembling, dense shrubbery and thick undergrowth awaited my eager hands. Dead wood snapped at a touch. Outstretched fingers pulled at thickets clinging to ancient trees, thorned vines stretched towards the silver sky. How my energy searched for something unknown! Suddenly, through webs of twisted prickly growth, my eyes faintly spied an ancient arch wide enough to crawl through.

How my excited hands freed brush and bramble! Animals, awakened from slumber, quickly scurried about. Ants blazed new trails. Crimson birds circled above, white butterflies fluttered. My determined body ached when I finally reached the arched entrance. And what awaited me? An abandoned cave whose roof curved with arched bricks. A grotto whose aged walls formed eight hollows, each with a weathered stone bench. Within its perfect center was a ninth hollow, a natural fountain with gushing water. Flowing from some hidden source, this vibrant spring swirled into an open basin. Bounded by moss and stones, its waters held a crystal pond clear enough for bathing.

Who had forsaken this mysterious cave? To whom had this sacred site belonged? Who had bathed in these waters of enchantment? Hours vanished as my body slipped naked into its crystal clear pond. Then did my dazzled mind hear spirits ancient and knowing. "Aisling," someone called, "Return to wild and savage rituals! Ecstatic maidens are dancing dreams by moonlight. Bonfires are brightly burning." Arising from these bubbling waters came visions of some eternal female power, fair as a full moon. Suddenly, stillness permeated the silver trees and swaying grass. The crystal waters settled into mirror brightness. Light waves shimmered upon its glass surface. Then did ancient voices softly speak, yet their words were bizarre and blurred. As I stepped from the cool waters, needle shivers ran across my arms. Could this have been a sacred site where a priestess once prophesized?

How these woodlands thrived from some strong female energy. In hours formless and free, spirals turned, released spirits caught in time. Multiple visions began to unfold. Excited feelings echoed the rhythms of nature. Here, far from restraints of home, my exuberant energy exploded! Something precious and primal penetrated my psyche. "Use your animal instinct, Aisling! Sense your way." Surely this voice belonged to the maiden with a silver bow and silver arrows. "Trust your intuition. Free your feelings. Become as alive as nature itself," she added.

How the surrounding silence shimmered, promising more to be revealed. Suddenly my spirit became self-centered. Then did I, Aisling, refuse to give myself to anyone but *me*. How my psyche guarded this serene space so nothing could intrude. Boundaries became clean and clear, defense of self became my strongest passion. My sexuality shielded any invasion into this virginal forest. Here my psyche heard voices, met energies never known before, discovered female dimensions near and far. In these woodlands an Aisling emerged who was outrageous and wild. Next to her stood the female of freedom, carrying a silver bow, shooting with straight arrows. Was she not a moonlit maiden, directing ritual dances with dignity and abandon? Covering her bare breasts with snakes and flowers, a maiden dedicated to being a virgin forever. A female of the forest whose moods changed from tension to release, tranquility to movement, resistance to surrender.

"Bend as a willow, be as bird!" was what the voice kept calling. Then did her energy ring crystal clear. "She who possesses rhythm, possesses the universe," she cheered. Was this huntress not a mixture of blood and will, chase and dance, scent and seeker? With rhythms soft, yet fierce as howling winds, how she commanded these rituals of reverie. "Use your newfound strength," she called. "Enact the dance of dreams with absolute attention. Discover secrets buried within woodlands and water." How my determination met her austere force. "Ease your perilous passage from one elated experience to the next," she shouted. "With jealousy protect your newfound intuition." Then did her fleeting form dart through trees, dance upon the bramble, and disappear as in a dream.

My sense of smell became acute, my self-preservation strong. Suddenly did I, Aisling, distance myself from myself, feeling this warrior energy expand. My awareness became astute, my vitality prevented any interference with this urgent force. The ancient cave became my womb of life, its waters my source of nourishment. Its gushing springs bathed me with inspiration. Yet from its strange presence arose an eerie curiosity. How my eyes peered into its waters for answers. How my psyche craved to unearth whatever lay deep beneath the mirror of this pond. From such sensations did my sixth sense surface.

Then did my psyche merge with the magic of myth. Clearly my mind had slipped far from the structure of society. Restrictions that had contained rebellion were released. Frustrations which had encouraged mutiny now dissolved. How the freedom of the forest seduced my head and heart! The control and constraint of home and school seemed another world. Yet had these limitations not prompted me to be expansive and daring? Had I needed to be confined in order to break out? From such boundaries had my wild wantonness fought its way clear. As my energy demanded change, so my psyche had shifted. My heart now reflected the rhythms of nature.

The adventure of risk held endless discovery, my freedom was bound by no one. In this atmosphere of aliveness, my attention extended everywhere, to the direction of the moon and every star. The East beckoning the coming spring, the South greeting the summer warmth. The West awakening autumn leaves, as the solitude of winter sought the North. Yet some strong force held back the winds, in-

35

spired sudden change. Was it the endless transformation of earth and sky, the birds and breezes never heard before?

How my search moved me towards the forces of freedom! Risk led me to the psychic edge of every cliff. Here my choices were to freeze or fly. Then did my heart explore woodlands sparkling with wonder. How shining stars fell at my feet! My hands held a magic wand, as flickering lights illuminated my path with silver radiance. Then did crystal waters of the pond entice me from these woodlands. Slowly did I succumb to an ancient memory of a miracle.

Gazing within these waters, the sun's reflection was never seen! Its glass surface mirrored only the silver crescent moon. Yet this mystical moon beckoned me to *see* what was not there. Images, evoking riddles of renewal, arose from its mysterious waters. The sliver of this silvery shape haunted me with feelings raw and untouched, its luminous light floating beneath these crystal waters. Drifting between secrets and shadows, forgotten parts of *me* returned. How my psyche wanted to tear apart my emotions, then put them back together again! How my mind prepared to help *me* become aware of myself. A strong hunger emerged for a new way of speaking. A deep desire surfaced for saying what my feelings really meant.

Running free through the forest my hair glistened with silver dust. My body darted graceful as a deer. Emotions expanded amidst blossoms and butterflies. Wildness burst with newly discovered potential. Unpredictable and excited, how my heart believed in my sudden strength! With closed eyes, arms outstretched, my body would spin around and around the crystal pond. Then my voice would chant:

Silver, Silver turn me round!
Silver, Silver touch my crown!
Silver, Silver reach my feet!
Silver, Silver fall as sleet!

Faster and faster did I turn, my mind twirling until dizziness ensued. Then did the ecstasy of a trance consume my psyche. How my body would fall upon the forest leaves. As my mind floated free, so scenes drifted as from dream to dream. Echoes of a voice, sounding as a priestess, faintly called. Only when twilight tones of sea green and sunset purple faded from sight did my five senses reawaken. Then my naked self once again plunged into the cave's cool waters. Refreshed, some semblance of reality returned to my psyche.

Only then did my mind and body rest. Yet my waking eyes would watch whatever images remained within the crystal waters. Strange visions often surfaced. Once, behind the silver moon, floated the trident from Captain Nodi's narrow boat, his lacy plates spinning in spirals. Sometimes castles and roses floated past my *sight.* Another time Ruby Red and Diamond White, in sparkling silver bubbles, dangled the world on a string. Only once did mad Medusa hold many mirrors as a mask. Often snakes surfaced staring into shining shields. Even a priestess of prophecy appeared, and a mystical queen who was a king.

Yet one vision would not dissolve. Within the willow tree, above the crystal pond, perched that capricious bird Urag. How he contemplated me with concern. How he watched my every movement. *Why* this creature hovered above the crystal waters was beyond my imagination. Even more disturbing, no reflection appeared upon the glassy surface. How could a bird exist without a shadow? The answer to this bizarre thought, my new self was soon to discover.

Suddenly silver eyes were beckoning me forth. How I felt
myself being watched!

The mirror revealed thoughts
hidden even to myself.

· VII ·
SILVER
SHADOWS

FOR NIGHTS THEREAFTER MY MIND SWAM through crystal waters. I, Aisling, could hardly sleep, tossing through the night, my thoughts turned into whirlpools of turmoil! Water and its vibrations floated through my body. Water stirring what appeared calm. Water opening faucets of feelings. Water, a looking glass mirror, inverting the order of things. Water, smoothing the hardest rock, overcoming and wearing down resistance. Was my psyche about to cross the stream? Enter another time frame? Discover a dimension of submerged wisdom, where memory drifted downwards into whirlpools of energy? Where spirits could purify and cleanse one's soul? Where my psyche might be tested by snake secrets of renewal and regeneration? Here past patterns could be washed away, present goals sanctified. Yet to dive into such waters meant to search for all things lost. Was my courage truly strong enough to change my mind?

Standing on this shadowy threshold, how its magical properties drew me closer. Within these waters awaited the mystical serpent queen, fabled to possess psychic powers over mortals. Here her mermaids lingered, divinities of water, tempters and seducers of men. Spirits, coming from primordial chaos, reflecting the turbulent forces of nature. Fearsome and terrifying, these undersea creatures challenged order and chaos, good and evil, light and darkness. Waves in ceaseless motion brought agitation, incited change. Troubled waters stirred pride and illusion. Was such action not churning my sleeping mind? Streaming like gushing water, chanting words for me to heed. How I listened to their meaning!

Water, water, luminous bright,
Bring her through the dark of night.

39

Take Aisling to the silver bubble.
Turn her towards the shimmering double.

Flowing water cursed to ice,
Light a frozen castle thrice.

And when white candles change to flame,
So shall her secret self return.

How my dream body twisted and turned upon itself. At last, with fingers out-stretched, my spirit glided towards an ocean of stars. Then, through the dimension of night, I could hear myself calling:

Souls of the Sea I cry through the night!
Hear me clearly! Heed my plight!

Guide me through this deep terrain
So my *sight* may return again.

Whatever fate shall await me thus
Know my heart holds infinite trust.

Whatever deeds you shall set forth
Aisling will heed at all costs.

Then did my sea water eyes search for the Kingdom under the Sea. Yet my dream body was gliding in the opposite direction, my psyche travelling, not through water, but through space. How swiftly was I passing meteors and moving planets. How bright were blinding beams of radiant light. Still my mind pounded with thoughts of water. Through images of gushing waves did my dream body try to swim. Finally, amidst torrential rains, my stubbornness succumbed to forces stronger than myself. And where did surrender take me? Far from the Kingdom under the Sea, instead to a luminescent silver bubble.

Yet only confusion and chaos awaited me. Fragments of smoky crystal burst in all directions, its splinters becoming crystal screens. How glass crashed, split, shattered through torrents of sound, as sonic waves thundered through my being! My dream body barely held together. Yet thoughts of water nearly drowned my mind. Urgently did one screen attract my attention, its blinking images appearing in reverse order. Then did my dream body fly above and below and around and behind, as my psyche tried to discover a view to be seen! Only after my mind bombarded its smoky glass did I safely arrive on the other side.

There a chorus called this revolving screen RORRIM, repeatedly chanting:

See how it glistens!
See how it shines!
See how it teases
What you call *time*!

Soprano voices sang in solo:

As dreams from RORRIM soon dissolve.
So dramas from its depths shall disappear.

Senseless sayings were sung. Then did a soprano voice exclaim, "Welcome to the bubble chamber of ERISED!" Then a second voice hailed, "Greetings beautiful RETAW!" Suddenly, sparkling on a glistening screen, loomed visions of Diamond White. Behind it the radiant moon brightly shimmered on still waters. How *seeing* the crystal pond upon the screen relaxed my being. Yet another female chorus burst forth, bringing further commotion and confusion.

May rivers cleanse you with clarity.
May streams flow through your heart.

May hurricanes keep you on course.
May your silver arrows fly steadfast.

When a sonorous voice proclaimed the name ERIF, then did my dream body tremble. Beams from Ruby Red spread red hot glows, the heat nearly scorching my soul! Only when my sense of suffocation ceased, did female voices chant again.

May flames of strength surround your sea of stars.
May fires of eternity carry you distant far.

May a full moon light your darkened way.
May a sparkling sun shine upon your face.

As fiery winds and watery voices sang like sirens, so RORRIM became an echo. Soon its sounds were indistinct. Then did these strange names from the silver bubble drift away. As vibrations of energy dissolved, intense heat left my body.

41

Crystal screens were no more. As my dream body faded, confusion changed to calm. Nothing lingered on the black velvet screen of my mind. Yet the sounds of the night haunted my memory in the morning.

Thereafter, when RORRIM resounded in my mind, something incredible happened. Sounding its name began to change my *sight*. Looking into the mirror my eyes beheld a vision unlike itself. The glass reflected my innermost secrets. The mirror revealed thoughts hidden even to myself. With the quality of a miracle, images transformed into a mysterious shadow. Were they perhaps forgotten scenes within my psyche? Yet, whenever these reflections appeared, the strange names from the SILVER DREAM were etched deeper in my mind.

How many nights this elusive voyage unfolded. Soon my dream body swam directly to ERISED. With fingers forward, feet outstretched, my mind arrived before a thought was finished. Always crystal screens, silent and serene, awaited my presence. A curious revolving chair stood before this wall of screens, made of solid silver, curved and molded, its shimmering surface awaited me. As my mind imagined *me* sitting in its silver frame, so my dream body slipped into its mould. Once encased within the shining chair, RORRIM pronounced either ERIF or RETAW, and the wall of crystal screens turned into either Ruby Red or Diamond White.

When Ruby Red replied, how ERIF clouded the screens with a hot current of air! Then were dark tunnels lighted by red glows. Stars blazed with fiery flames, as male voices repeated the name ERIF, and crystal screens exploded from intense heat. Planets collided, stars disintegrated, splinters of meteors crashed through the sky. Worlds unknown burst before my eyes. "Hold onto your silver seat!" ERIF shouted as the journey into chaos began, and the rage of wrath exploded all emotions! Thrust by the current of opposing forces, so my dream body spun and whirled. Tornadoes sent me into spirals of confusion. Roaring winds and fierce heat penetrated whatever was left of my mind.

As thunder bombarded my thoughts, so ERIF remained constant. Then did lightning streaks flash through my mind. Winds of night blew my psyche asunder. Fragments of my former self burst as meteors themselves. Only the strength of clarity saved me from the chaos of ERIF. Then, as my dream body succumbed to these storms, so the ashes of ERIF blew into the galaxy. A hushed silence followed. Air and space became so quiet that the fluttering of night wings could be heard. Why then, coming from this strange stillness, did cries of a wolf curl through my mind? Eerie sounds which encircled my senses with a glow of crimson red.

Suddenly, the silver chair began to spin. When it stopped, my mind was startled by ERISED, and the wall of crystal screens abounded with multiple images of myself! Visions of *me* floating through the universe. On one screen, seen through waves of lime green light, drifted my physical body. Another showed my shadow

42

self asleep within the silver chair. Yet a third screen presented my dream body propelled by ERIF into space, and a fourth mirrored my light body shimmering in reflections of RETAW. Infinite images of myself moved on every crystal screen. How my sense of self was shattered! Was nothing about *me* unique?

How ERISED lured me to follow RETAW through this voyage into seas of darkness. First came a floating feeling, then a sequence like a stream. Clear bubbles sparkled with silver lights. My mind swam through whirlpools of water, as tides of the silver moon carried my dream body into this subterranean world. Here answers were offered as questions. Riddles without rhyme appeared to have no reason. Yet something within my psyche floated free and clear, my empty mind receptive to whatever flowed forth.

How RETAW enticed me to realms beneath the sea! On many crystal screens my shadow self watched my dream self swim through ink black waters. Yet nothing disturbed my voyage, not fearsome waves nor shrill calls of sea monsters who dwelt in lakes of evil. How my eyes avoided females with long green fangs and dark green teeth. Did they not lurk below stagnant, moss covered rocks? Tangled amidst seaweed, their green hair ensnared whatever came within their grasp. With courage did my dream self focus upon deep turquoise and emerald waters. There within were coral fans and white sands, jewels of diamond white. Were these mystical riches not known throughout the world of myth?

Then the silver chair revolved again, rotating my shadow self to another crystal screen. Dazzling my mind, so it revealed the hidden source of prophecy. Why the gift of crystal clarity was bestowed upon each priestess in ancient times! The ability to *see* beyond limits of time and space. In the far distance, appeared a fifth me, now truly Aisling of the dream. Yet why was this spirit body clothed in robes of white, bands of jewelled snakes upon its arms? "You are to meet the Serpent Queen. The one who dwells amidst snakes, protecting the secrets of life," were the words that flowed through the waters. How RETAW then guided me through this subterranean current. Lapping rhythms of the sea became sounds to heed. Mermaids called clear truths, "Water responds in the way that it must," one female voice exclaimed. My intuition sensed fingers caressing a crystal water jug. "See how water is contained before its powers are released!" called another voice.

Suddenly silver eyes were beckoning me forth. How I felt myself being watched! Yet only shadows now slid beneath the sonorous sea. In these depths of darkness my mind could *see* no more. Slowly did RETAW fade from the crystal screen. Then did my shadow body slip from the silver chair. Drifting past the night, so my dream journey dissolved. As morning awakened my tunnel eyes, worlds of learning never left my thoughts. Yet how my waking mind needed to unravel these mysteries. Then did it seem that RORRIM reflected whatever was before my eyes.

Had ERISED not enticed me to follow my instincts? Surely ERIF offered voyages through air and space. Had RETAW not enchanted me with a Kingdom beneath crystal waters?

Now, before the slumbers of each night, my heart was anxious. Only through the sixth sense of *sight* could these voyages be fathomed. How my rational mind was concerned. How my sense of self felt threatened. For where might these night lessons lead me next?

Snake visions would
coil around her hair,
caged within the memory of her mind.

· VIII ·
MIND
MIRRORS

VIVIENNE TOSSED AND TURNED through the night. In the morning she always felt as if a sledge hammer had been beating at her head. Tension headaches had plagued her as long as she could remember. They seemed part of her life. The pounding pressure came from images in her mind that she dare not express, scenes that crowded one upon the other. Visions she never expressed or released. Each day began with disoriented feelings, not being able to unlock the throbbing inside her head. Thumping sounds, dark thuds, pressed against her brow. Sometimes a cool, wet cloth relieved the pressure. Other times, her closed eyes were mesmerized by flashing electric streaks darting across her brain. Waves of current would streak through her mind, an eternal parade of lightning shocks and peacock colors, static movements and bursting sparks. That she managed to meet the morning school bus was her personal miracle.

Her porcelain facade masked this inner turmoil. Red gold hair and sea green eyes attracted instant attention. Faraway stares and complacent smiles removed her from present time. Photographers asked her to pose, and artists wanted to paint her portrait. Pre-Raphaelite was how they described her pallid skin and savage hair. Frequently, to their surprise, Vivienne accepted. Her reward was an abundance of attention mingled with the solitude of success. How she thrived in the tranquillity of a photography studio! Classical music floated through the air. A single white lily would fill a nearby vase. A perfect green grape might be peeled for her amusement.

Vivienne could pose for hours in an atmosphere of serenity. Yet not one soul knew her Scorpio secret. These clandestine sessions always were after school. Then did her fantasy flow, in the mystical hours between late afternoon and sunset. As the sun faded, so the palette of the world changed. Dusk would begin, that mysterious time when the sky turned somber and serene. Praised as the painter's light, its warm glow awakened her sensuality. Vivienne would await its elusiveness.

The silence of these sessions suited Vivienne well. She never did care for conversation. Words to express her thoughts were difficult to find, so many images jumbled together. Visions too vibrant for sentences to describe. Nothing ever came out clear. Although her mind listened well, these secret fears separated Vivienne from others. Classmates called her exotic, elusive, enchanting. Only part of this was true. Vivienne was simply frightened, her soul and personality in mortal combat.

Her attraction to Aisling was not surprising, she had been observing her for a long while. Drawn towards her drifting eyes, her distant manner intrigued Vivienne. Rumors and remarks never disturbed Aisling's inner quiet. Yet, unlike Vivienne, her reserve seemed more remote, although she appeared satisfied and secure. Vivienne watched and wondered. How often she would see Aisling walking alone in school corridors, pretending no one else was present. Lost in thought, books in hand, she was drifting through worlds of her own. Never was Aisling where others gathered to gossip. Instead, she was always seen leaving for the library. Her avid reading, thinking, silent scribbling, made Vivienne believe Aisling must be involved in something special.

Vivienne was more than curious. What was Aisling searching for? Why was she reading endless books? Intensity attracted Vivienne, she was drawn towards eccentric ways. Aisling was courageous enough to be separate. Yet might they not be similar? Each one calm on the surface while seething within? Willful, obsessive, self-reliant. Distant while needing a friend. How much courage it had taken for Vivienne to sit beside Aisling on the school bus. How many curious eyes had been upon them. How many whispers had wandered through the school corridors. Yet their first conversation had piqued, but not pleased, one another.

Vivienne's private passion was collecting mirrors, her bedroom walls patterned with bizarre shapes found in exotic places. Hand mirrors, framed mirrors, concave mirrors, convex mirrors. The more curious the looking glass, the stronger her desire for possession. Mirrors made Vivienne's mind dazzle and dance. The sun shining upon their surfaces cast iridescent sparkles on her bedroom walls. The silver glow of moonlight made them elusive and suggestive. Dusk was when Vivienne felt their soft magic. Then did her mirrors have the quality of a miracle. To Vivienne, the mirrored image had a reality of its own, returning a reflection of her shadow. Vivienne thought this a likeness of her soul that the mirror possessed—magical qualities, making her a shadow-holder. Hidden parts of her unconscious became visible. Yet she could only glean indirect conclusions about these reflections. The elusiveness of its mystery appealed to her surreal nature. Mirrors made Vivienne conscious that everything was a reflection of her innermost thoughts.

The mirror which Vivienne cherished most was kept beside her bed. Carved

46

D*id the mirrors of water not reflect one's inner self?*

upon its frame, a magical blue and red bird was surrounded by sensuous snakes. Vivienne pretended this mythical creature, with red gems for eyes, held ancient charms. Its silent stare concealed secrets waiting to be revealed. She imagined the mirror to possess powers of long ago. How it would reflect the wonder of a white flying horse, the splendor of a golden sword with brilliant jewels! Then, gazing into these gems, her sea green eyes would dazzle with sparkling lights and glittering colors. Through these translucent jewels, she would swim past burning candles, smell the scent of cinnamon, hear music through rushing waves. Strangely would she recall fire torches, silver ribbons tied to forest trees.

None of this dare she speak. Vivienne held the fabric of fate close to her soul. How often this bedside mirror portrayed her in silks of black and gold, silver threads sewn with lustrous pearls of white. To share such secrets seemed a Cassandra curse in time. Yet this mirror left her obsessed with her red gold hair. Henna hair symbolized thoughts, guarded the secrets held within her head. Their strands sheltered her mind from invasion and intrusion. Vivienne was aware that possessing another's locks meant psychic power over them! Thus did she protect herself. Flowing hair was a sign of freedom, energy, strength. Her desire to succeed. Consciously did Vivienne wear her red gold hair as a magical headdress. Did females in former times not carry the symbols of their souls upon their heads?

Yet what frightened Vivienne was when this bedside mirror reflected darkness and despair. Then would snakes invade her bounteous hair, her beauty turning into serpent curls. How her mind writhed with dark and primitive emotions. Then, thoughts which seemed not her own, would surface. Conflicting feelings brought an energy with the dread of death. During such moments Vivienne felt possessed. Snake visions would coil around her hair, caged within the memory of her mind. When serpentine scenes flashed before her mirror eyes, then did Vivienne suffer the pounding pressure that brought the dreaded darkness to her brain.

Seated before the dressing table mirror, slowly did she brush her abundant hair. How she longed for a trustworthy friend, someone with whom these submerged secrets could be shared. Only Aisling had potential, how often she seemed to mirror her mind. Yet what bizarre comments had come from her whenever Vivienne chose not to reply. Her sentences had seemed strange indeed. Then would Vivienne feel Aisling had been an oracle in ancient times. With such foolish thoughts in mind, she shook her hair loose from the brush. Then, without reason, Vivienne looked at her hand.

There, reflected upon her palm, was a deep sapphire gem, an ancient stone known to heal both mind and spirit. A powerful gem whose vibrations enhanced intuition and insight. How its electric blue rays sent tingles across her flesh! Yet no other shade but its own was reflected. Was this strange sign confirming her feelings about Aisling? As if rising from beneath the sea, its deep brilliance hinted at the mysteries of truth and trust. Then did Vivienne consider something curious. Could such a sapphire stone unlock psychic thoughts within her pulsing mind? Might such a jewel symbolize hidden treasures of knowledge, wisdom from beyond?

This thought prompted images of stagnant and still waters. Suddenly Vivienne sensed something imprisoned that needed to be freed. Flowing waters of life coursed through her mind. Yet another vision appeared, seen in three parts. First she watched a black lethal scorpion, craving the pleasure of stinging. Suddenly it stung itself to death. Vivienne, a Scorpio by birth, cringed. Second, an eagle flew closer to the sun than any other bird. And last, a phoenix was resurrected from the ashes of its dead self. In that strange second the sapphire light faded from her hand. Then did the dressing table mirror reveal a brilliant red light. After that, nothing more was seen.

Vivienne was relieved. Her cluttered mind could not contain another thought. Still her feelings became excited. Inspired, she decided to connect with Aisling again. This time, however, Vivienne prepared herself to speak the truth.

"How much longer must we battle my friend?
Shall our warring never end?"

· IX ·

CAPTAIN NODI

CAPTAIN NODI BELLY LAUGHED ALOUD, so pleased with himself. Finally he had caught Aisling, trapped in the net he had set. How long had this one taken? Years? Centuries? Infinity? What a scathing sea voyage it had been. What an obstinate female to be tested and taught! Captain Nodi heaved a heavy sigh, "Oh, well, other assignments have been worse." Then his mind drifted out to sea. "At least this one is curious," he mumbled to himself. "Star clusters still swimming in her eyes."

How often had he found himself musing about Aisling, thinking of her flittering hither and fro, racing from century to century, not keeping any dimension in order. What worlds had she wandered through! What personalities had she awakened from the past? What fables had she found in future time? How could his mind possibly unravel what Aisling already had scrambled? Was it any wonder that her life seemed out of sorts? Clearly she was everywhere and nowhere at once, never remaining long enough to see what was happening. Too busy exploring lifetimes gone by. Seeking dimensions not yet disclosed, discovering atmospheres too rarefied to enter. "Oh, well," Captain Nodi muttered to himself, "Maybe this one will serve me to settle some old scores."

Then did he strike a match and light the oven to toast yesterday's bread. Captain Nodi turned on the burner to make freshly brewed coffee. "Only way to start a brisk Autumn day," he murmured to himself. Fondly did he finger the old chipped mug, "Been around for ages, eh what? Just like me." With steaming coffee cup in hand, he slowly sauntered through the narrow cabins, then went above board. Taking care on the slippery steps, his feet pushed aside scattered yellow leaves. Dewdrops dampened his red geraniums, and moisture on the brightly painted tiller felt cool to his hands. In the morning mist there were few distractions but his churning

49

thoughts. Fog made Captain Nodi relax. Humidity helped him breathe better. Some people lived on air. He thrived on water, no matter what its form.

Certainly all seemed peaceful and in place. Then why was his mood so irritable, his feelings so restless? The answer came in an instant. Why that insufferable bird Urag! His brass cage was empty. Where had that cantankerous creature gone? Captain Nodi was exasperated. How often had his golden chariot raced through the sky to find that bird? How many times had his white stallions coaxed Urag home again? "Exhausting that one," he grumbled to himself, "Too invisible for his own good."

Hot coffee usually soothed his soft belly. Not today. With heavy sighs his mind returned to Aisling. Sensations of annoyance arose, and suddenly he shouted aloud. "When will Aisling learn to listen? When will she stay still? Where is she wandering now? Why has she not returned to me?" Impulsively, his eyes gleamed with delight. Straightaway Captain Nodi decided to alter his form. Just a fraction. Stir her memory a bit. "Might even help her remember when last we met!" Yes, he would make himself taller, leaner, a touch lustful. Faded blue jeans, worn yellow slicker, white hair combed crisp, white Captain's cap. Might even suggest a secret rendezvous in a sacred place beneath the sea. No more "Old Man of the Sea" stuff. Wiping his brow, Captain Nodi grinned with pleasure. Time to get Aisling out of her head and into her heart.

Once again did he praise himself, pleased with his voyage of enticement. Now where should this scene be set? Below the ocean depths? Beyond rainfalls and storms? Before streams and waterfalls? Past rapids and torrents, floods and hurricanes? Which route would satisfy his sense of style? Which would entice her mind, body, *and* spirit? Surely this was a task worthy of a god. Suddenly his eyes narrowed. No, he thought, he would play his cards as they came. A provoker at heart, Captain Nodi preferred risk to strategy. Never before had he charted a course to be taken. His moods rolled with the waves, blew as tornadoes, ignited as lightning storms. Impetuously, he stalked around in stormy rages or slowly sauntered, tranquil as a moonlit lake. Only that annoying bird Urag eluded him. "Now where has he flown this time?" So irritated thoughts began again.

Anger kept Captain Nodi from savoring the fresh moist morning air. He counted on his fingers again and again. How many moments, minutes, months had his sapphire wings been gone? Then did he grit his teeth. "Why doesn't the *time of day* bother that maddening bird?" he bellowed. His mind was tired of this trouble. Crimson feathers had to be hovering about. His twinkling eyes searched the skies as his annoyance mounted. Yet naught was found. "Urag!" he shouted, "Answer me, now! I command you at once!" Not a whisper was heard. Then did Captain Nodi make a drastic decision. His temper would call forth tempests and tornadoes, his rage would release chaos and commotion. Confusion would create endless calamity.

Effusive emotions knew no truth but his own.

Gathering wits and wile, with wrathfulness did this rampage begin. The seas darkened. Thunder shook the earth. Lightning thwarted the sky. Cyclones unfurled, trees tore asunder. Clouds provoked torrential tides. Canals began to churn, and the narrow boat Nebulae rolled from side to side. Waves pushed its painted hull from shore to shore. Drawers slid along the cabin floor. Copper pots fell from above the blackened stove and plates knocked against oak walls. The brass bell clanged for help, yet no one answered its call. Captain Nodi, too engrossed, savored his coming success. Once more did he storm past the empty brass cage, shouting loudly, "In one second of time, victory will be mine!"

Abruptly, before blinking his eyes, success *was* his. Familiar screeching sounded above the upper deck, as fluttering filled the narrow cabins below. Urag shouted his rage. "Has madness made you a maniac? Has your brain gone berserk? What in Heaven are you doing?" How this creature detested calamity! Captain Nodi, however, glowered without mercy, crying, "So rough winds blew you home! So the sea almost made you sink!" Then did the bird's fierce eyes narrow, as he thought to flee again. Instead, slowly, did he reply, "How much longer must we battle my friend? Shall our warring never end?" Turning away, exhausted, his sapphire wings folded beneath soft crimson feathers. Then did his golden beak close to sleep. "Oh, no you don't!" Captain Nodi hollered, "Not that trick! Not that one again! Too long have you been gone!" Seizing his silver trident from behind the blackened stove, Captain Nodi stood with legs astride, and glared into the cage of brass. No peace was possible until Urag confessed *where* he had been, *what* he had seen, *why* he had disappeared.

Instead, the bird yawned brilliant bubbles of radiant light. How the narrow boat blazed with sparkling beams, drowning all disturbances. Captain Nodi stood speechless. Why, bursting from these bubbles, floated Ruby Red and Diamond White! Surely the battle had begun. Only then did Captain Nodi hold his tongue, while Urag smiled a secret smirk. Yet stillness surrounded their searching eyes. Three times around Urag did Ruby Red weave a web of crimson light. Then three times did Diamond White encircle Captain Nodi with beams of crystal white. Clear voices rang with crystal tones! "Soon shall we turn the tides of time!" they declared.

Suddenly, as if performing a sacred rite, together they decreed:

May restful seas reflect the radiant sun!
May many moons meet the mountain peaks!

May lakes and clouds form to flow as one!
May Mother Earth unite with Father Sky!

Immediately the boatman's cabin filled with brilliant ribbons. Vibrant colors dissolved, then disappeared. Now, next to Captain Nodi stood the shadow of Aisling, crystal white and virgin pure. Behind Urag awaited the outline of Geraint, a hero with crimson tunic and golden sword. Beyond the brass portholes infinite worlds of night and day spun into one deep dream. Visions arose of vistas yet unknown. "From turnings in twilight time come the making of myths!" cried the crystal voices of Ruby Red and Diamond White. Then they disappeared.

Yet all of this seemed so ancient. Were these not patterns repeating themselves? How many times had Diamond White merged with Captain Nodi through waters bright with light? How often had radiant rays of Ruby Red flown Urag to the glowing sun? In the still silence of space, atoms and molecules shifted as specks of dazzling dust. Surely the unexpected was about to begin. Suddenly a reverse spin turned Nebulae upon itself, and in that strained second of stillness not one shadow touched another.

Then was Aisling standing with her feet firm upon the ground, while the shadow of Geraint was drifting through darkened seas. The narrow boat Nebulae spiralled beneath the sea itself. No longer were there bird songs and bluebells. No flowering branches laden with blossoms rested upon cool waters. No winds caught the canal boat as it calmly moved along. Suddenly they seemed enveloped by the sea itself. Still Captain Nodi held the tiller to keep the butty's bow in line. And why did his smile applaud where they had just arrived?

Huddled in the corner of his brass cage, Urag began to shudder and shake. His crimson feathers dreaded this "Kingdom under the Sea"! Through the portholes his piercing eyes had seen enough. There were silver mermaids with serpent tails instead of legs and castles made of frozen ice that never thawed! Treasures of wealth and wisdom none could ever touch. How Urag dreaded the fearsome powers of the sea. His frightened feathers could not fly away. Trapped by forces of terrestrial tides, terror near stopped his beating heart. His sapphire wings felt bound by a whirlpool of rage, caught in an ocean of anger.

Urag tucked his head into his crimson breast. His feathered face collapsed in confusion. "Oh no, no, no!" he wailed, shaking his head in disbelief. Beneath the sea his beloved sun disappeared into darkness. Soon the psychic Serpent Queen Agan would spin her silver threads around his secret golden wings. How he dreaded the sea which reflected the starkness of the moon. How he feared dark waters ruled by female forces! Here silver mermaids, through tests and trials, tempted one towards treasures of the Sea. Adorned with slithering serpents, they protected the psychic powers of the night! Threatened by instinct and intuition, Urag craved the masculine light of day.

Buried within these depths of dreams were memories Urag did not want divulged. The forgotten was exactly what he feared. Whatever dissolved in the waters of emotions was well dismissed. Whatever floated above should drown in its labyrinths of loss. Was the fire of his flaming sun not dampened by the sea of souls? Were his soaring wings not submerged by waves of water? Were death and dreams not the same, both ruled by the tunnels of the night? Yet, sadly, did he succumb to the shadows of the sea.

Captain Nodi, however, blossomed beneath the tides. Female energy restored in his memory a paradise of peace. To him the womb was wondrous. How many enchanting maidens had seduced souls seeking these darkened waters. How silver mermaids had graced the seas and moisture of the soil! Deftly had they lured those who sought the life beyond. How often had Captain Nodi seen such beauteous beings swim upon the shore. How he had watched them search for shining lights around the seeker's face, as shadows flickered from beyond. With swiftness did the magic mermaids seduce anyone who dared return to realms unknown.

How often had Captain Nodi crossed the stream into this immortal zone. Delighted by their dazzle, he dreamt the many ways a silver mermaid might tempt and tantalize his mind. How she would flirt and twist her teasing tail, shimmer the metallic scales upon her form. Mesmerize him with magic to behold. And all because this Kingdom brought good luck, prosperity, great fortune incarnate. Such timeless thoughts, however, were stopped by siren sounds coming from the sea.

"Greetings to Captain Nodi!" called a voice of silver dust, "Remember me? The one you dared to trust!" To which he smiled and said, "Ah, the magnificent maiden with the silver tail, the slippery one who never fails!" So did the silver mermaid swish her fins for him. Then did she think to fall into his arms, meaning no malicious harm. But Captain Nodi kept his distance. "The battle has begun!" he said, "Take me to your mystic Queen!" Yet, without a sign, the merry maiden disappeared from sight. Only lascivious laughter rang throughout the silent sea.

Abandoned by this mercurial mermaid, Captain Nodi feared not that he could find his way alone. How often had he travelled to this Kingdom below the Sea! This realm of hidden treasures, secrets not a soul beheld. Then pensively did he ponder to himself, "How long has it been since last I saw the psychic Serpent Queen Agan?" With fondness did he recall the regal Queen with hood of serpent heads. The turquoise amulets on her upper arms, the glistening bracelets loose upon her wrists. Her tunnel eyes that told she alone was mistress of the sea, maintainer of the earth itself. Yet never had her shield of shimmering snakes troubled Captain Nodi. How he had honored these guardian snakes who held the ancient records of past and future times. How their wisdom eye preserved both jewels and metals of the earth. Did their deadly poison not protect her riches—difficult to reach, dangerous to find?

Yet for Captain Nodi the sea was seductive more than secret. Its waters whispered, its waves inviting his soul to wander in a spell of solitude. Here, in mazes of memory, were all cares lost. Here, through contemplation, did visions arise. Yet how many questions awaited answers. "Perhaps," thought he, "it might be best to offer gifts before greeting Queen Agan again." Thus did Captain Nodi bestow upon her seas perfumed fragrance and scented flowers. He sprinkled her waves with sandalwood powder, ointments from rose petals, essences nurtured by those divine. Then did he think, "Perhaps these scents shall reach the riches at the bottom of her sea!" How these treasures tempted him! Captain Nodi always wondered what secrets of creation lay beneath all chaos and confusion. Surely the depth of the sea mirrored segments of the psyche never seen before. Thoughts which might divulge where treasures would be hidden. Thus was Captain Nodi willing to dive into experience, swim with uncertainty. Had unceasing waves not always turned his thoughts around?

Captain Nodi knew that psychic Queen Agan could *see* all wisdom and all wrath! Her sea-bound sleep brought crystal dreams, the counterpart of light. Her visions watched him well. She chose, however, not to welcome Captain Nodi of the narrow boat Nebulae. "No," thought she, "his cluster of stars will have to wait." Thus did the elusive Serpent Queen prepare for peace. How past problems drifted through her mind, as endless waves of memory brought seas of trust ignored. With prudence did the Serpent Queen of *sight* decide to stay detached. Yet had the time not come to right so many wrongs? How long had her silver serpents clashed with Urag of the golden wings? Had this not begun before the beginning of time itself? How often had his sun parched her sacred soil, dried up the moisture of life? Swallowed sea waters which lay upon her Earth. Scorched her serpentine rivers potent with snakes and tried to end the power of her *sight*.

Had Urag of Heaven not challenged the Earth and Sea? Her Kingdom hidden in hollows below the soil, nourishing all seas of life. Her domain which thrived on the waters of emotion. Celestial Urag breathed the breath of boundless air, while serpent tails were water bound. Never could Queen Agan rise as an eagle in the sky, soar through limitless space, reach the timeless sphere beyond the stars. Only her psyche could penetrate this realm. Her strength lay beneath the earth, within the wisdom of the water. Did her mystery not rule the great Sea upon which the Earth rested?

Now must the Serpent Queen of *sight* forgive in order to forget. Her snake skins shed themselves once more. Wash away the old, sanctify the new. Such powers purified and cleansed, regenerating those who wished to start again. Feelings of fear must cease. Intuition needed to increase. Had the knowledge of her Kingdom not saved the source of the shadow? The fountain of the spring, emerging from emotions, refreshing the soul itself. Did such feelings not flow as waves through water?

Cowering within his cage of brass, Urag pretended not to heed these potent

*Captain Nodi knew that psychic Queen Agan could see all wisdom
and all wrath! Her sea-bound sleep brought crystal dreams,
the counterpart of light.*

thoughts! Danger and disaster streamed through his mind. Too frightened to dream, he stayed awake. How he feared this subterranean current which changed endlessly. Never did he want to weave through its waves, nor be trapped in the intoxication of its trance. Not once had his shadow separated from the sunshine of his soul. Yet now the depths of dreams brought disturbance to his days. Here in the sea of souls rested the source of all prophecy. The ability to *see* phenomena from beyond. Yet none of this helped his present plight. Nor did he know *what* and *how* to fight.

Urag was not the only one disturbed. Pensively, Captain Nodi brewed his breakfast coffee on the blackened stove. Why was he scratching his head, staring into the surrounding sea? Surely his thoughts had drifted away, and the current was moving them in directions even he could not predict. How often had he commanded these tides, rode its churning waves, strode upon this sea! Destructive waters were dark, dangerous, deceitful. Calm waters brought forth instinct, intuition, insight. Yet had Captain Nodi not seen a vision which disturbed? Two serpents entwined in amorous embrace, their heads not facing one another. Had each not worn a crown with a sea of stars? Yet *why* had both reflected sun and moon apart?

Captain Nodi shook his head, thinking that this vision might dissolve. Perhaps his perfumed scents had been too strong. Urag was still tucked within his sapphire wings, soundly sleeping in his cage of brass. Nothing seemed changed. Suddenly Captain Nodi chuckled to himself, no more need he pretend. Then did his body plunge into the cool and unhurried reaches of the water, as strange thoughts surfaced. "Were divinities of water, living beneath the Sea, not gifted with powers of prophecy?" Then did the echo of Urag's voice resound. Surely he had rebutted, "Were divinities of air, living above in Heaven, not blessed with the potency of prayer?"

Captain Nodi shook the churning waves from his mind. Swiftly did he swim further into the depths of the surging sea. He had decided to seek the mystical Queen Agan with haste. With crystal clarity he realized there was much for them to discuss.

The feminine eye which could see
all things unseen.

· X ·

ENERGY ERUPTS

THE CLOTHES IN MY WARDROBE WERE SHUFFLED, a different palette now hung where my hands could reach. It did not matter that my skirts and shirts were fewer. Rather I, Aisling, was concerned about their reflection. Instinct told me to wear earth brown, soft coral, moss green, sea blue, deep purple. Shades that reflected intuition, imagination, instinct. Colors that penetrated the vibrations of nature. Tones that blended with water and woodlands. Feelings that enhanced my insight, protected my psyche, shared my secrets. Reflections that made me vulnerable, increased my aliveness, added to my awareness.

Why then did my dreams always dress me in white with cloak of blue, silver stars within my flowing hair? Clearly no classmate would understand my need to know these answers. How I, Aisling, spent infinite hours in the school library. Endless books described colors connected to the elements of earth, air, fire, water. Yet first my curiosity craved to know all about red and white, to help explain the strange vibrations of Ruby Red and Diamond White. Then did my mind search library stacks to discover details about gold and silver. How I suspected gold to be connected to that strange creature Urag, as silver belonged to the serpent Queen Agan.

Yet books not only linked colors with elements, but with mysterious myths about the North, South, East, West. The more I read, so further thoughts popped into my head. How the rays of Ruby Red came from the East, sparkled with the flames of fire. Surely these vibrations were masculine, their color the warmth of the sun. The physical energy of blood, linking all levels of life. Might its vibrations then bring health and vigor, friendship and love? Could Geraint be its hero? How often in my dreams had he worn the color of warrior red, the gold of the glistening sun. Were his snake tanks not facing East, watching the dawn? "Might then he seek conquest through willpower, seduction through lust?" flashed a frantic thought in my head.

57

How I cowered from such a concept. Was red not worn by victors and emperors alike, a symbol of royalty itself? Clearly such flames inspired Geraint's quest in life.

Yet did this energy not also symbolize the sacred? How Scorpio Vivienne praised the Phoenix who arose from flames of fire! Was Urag not always escaping, trying to fly to the golden sun? How many books described ancient rites which used torches, bonfires, burning embers. How often initiation dreams were dreams of fire. Then did I remember sitting before the fire in Father's library. Had my *sight* not seen infinite images in the flames? Yet, how a red roaring fire frightened me! Was that why Ruby Red disturbed my dreams?

Surely the brilliance of white belonged to water. Did it not come from the cold darkness of the North? The land of night, winter white, shining by the light of the moon. The feminine eye which could *see* all things unseen. Did Diamond White not nourish the birth of the new, honor the death of the old? Was white not the color of purity, innocence, chastity? The beginning of all beginnings? Did not the tides of water heed the mother moon? Was her realm not intuition, imagination, insight? Here abounded symbols of silver and quicksilver, myths of snakes and serpents, tales of leaving illusion to enter the clarity of crystal. Did the mirrors of water not reflect one's inner self? Might this be the treasure beneath the sea? Had the psychic Queen Agan shared her secrets with the dreams of Diamond White?

Slowly did my mind unravel the web of threads spun around me. With care, the tapestry of my thoughts wove together. Clearly Diamond White had brought my Silver Dreams, shown me the mysteries of silver and snakes. Then had Ruby Red, with flames of fire, brought chaos and confusion, passion and power. Yet could these opposites not meet, perhaps unite with one another? Pondering such thoughts, deep in concentration, nothing around me seemed to exist. Students passing before my desk were hardly noticed. Only when thinking of Ruby Red did my head unexpectedly raise. And who should be standing there? Why none other than blue eyed, black haired Geraint! My emotions dove under the sea. My mind near floated away. Yet, still, his strained voice reached me.

"Excuse me for interrupting," his awkward words began. "Remember me? You visited our house one Sunday afternoon for tea." Did my mind remember? How many days and nights had Geraint exhausted my thoughts. Why, having finally dismissed him, did he suddenly appear, a blaze of fire red surrounding his face? Was Geraint aflame with the heat of the sun, the glow of warmth? How my thoughts secretly smiled! "Perhaps he has come from the East of passions and perceptions." Yet how suspect were his impulsive charms and effusive manners. How awkward to see him again. "Just wondered if you'd like to take a break!" he exclaimed. His casual words sounded contrived. "You have a lot of books there!" he continued, unabated. Squirming in my chair, my suspicions surprised me. Did my present resistance not become stronger than my past attraction? Something potent warned me to protect myself. His casualness alerted my caution, as my mind measured his words.

Surely months had passed since that Sunday afternoon. Clearly his avoidance had moved me toward other actions. Had his withdrawal not made me assert myself? His withholding increased my inner strength. Only the shadow of his secret self poised as a question mark in space. Yet how his blue eyes narrowed. His restless hands moist within his pockets, a studied smile that never left his face. Indeed, Geraint wanted something. Yet my intuition could not determine *what*. With animal instinct my mind studied him with pointed concentration.

Only friendship could my heart conceive. Some equal sharing of inspiration, perhaps searching the curious snake energy we held together. That, however, meant admitting having seen his wriggling snakes. Instantly my primary concern was for psychic protection. My intuition sensed Geraint to be dangerous and determined. Did his presence not seem anxious? His attention too razor sharp? A tenacity that came from a clear decision that required a precise result. Yet his vibrations offered neither a second chance nor a second thought!

Intrigued by his electric blue eyes, my fantasy and frivolity decided to forgive. Perhaps his masculine heat appealed to my feminine heart. Then, in that flash of a thought, did everything turn upon itself. Why suddenly, through Geraint's eyes, did I hear his voice? As he walked away, his words came closer. Hidden hands appeared to point the way. The desk before me disappeared, note papers blew about, fell into Geraint's outstretched hands. Books before me closed, then opened to different pages. Yet, through this turmoil sounded the cries of a wolf. Then the hissing of snakes. Was the strength of the sun, rising at dawn, bombarding my vision? All had happened without a breeze or breath. No one but I, Aisling, had witnessed these scenes.

Yet within seconds did these visions fade. Turning my head, the library scene returned to my sight. Although my throat trembled, my words sounded strong. "No! No, thank you! I don't need a break!" came my reply. "And yes, of course, I recognize you!" my jeering eyes answered. Rather than being disgruntled, Geraint's tongue tasted the spice. "You intrigue me more, Aisling! Now that you're unavailable!" To which he slowly appended, "Do call me when you want to talk about snakes!" Then Geraint turned and stalked away. Yet *the huntress one must hunt* had no intention of following the wrath of red.

After several deep breaths my composure was restored. Yet again had his energy disturbed me. What had prompted Geraint to appear? Surely what seemed sudden impulse came from calculated risk. Feelings, which had been calm and self-assured, now churned. The center of my psyche wobbled in all directions. How my heart refused to relax! Fire red colors flashed before my eyes. Disconnected, once again did my mind leap from my body. The face of Geraint became a silver mirror.

59

My psyche stared at strange scenes which suddenly appeared. There were ritual scenes in the woodlands. Candles blazing around a circular shimmering lake. Into its shining surface an ancient priestess gazed, wearing virgin white, softly did she speak of things to come. The moonlit forest meshed strange magic with mystery. Rays of white light streamed from the priestess of prophecy to spirits below the glistening waters. Then did the stillness of the scene awaken with life. Snakes surfaced from the lake, coiled around branches, hissing with waiting tongues. Crystal waters glistened from the light of the moon. Scenes surfaced, then dissolved. Not another word was spoken. The priestess closed her water eyes, immersed in deep slumber. Softly did the snakes retreat to whence they came. Flames of red then clouded the silver mirror, and amidst this raging fire, nothing more was seen.

Slowly my focus returned to the library scene. Yet, after clearing my head, agitated thoughts arose. How my senses shouted! "Mirrors! Mirrors! How they plague my mind!" All I could think about were mirrors which turned upside down and inside out. Mirrors where walking forwards was looking backwards. The Looking Glass Mirror. The Looking Glass House. Alice on the Other Side. Mirrors where objects went another way. How in mirrors my body would travel away from me, and my sanity would seem insane! Mirrors where everything revolved in reverse order. The familiar world, changed and distorted, became another existence. Whatever felt familiar turned into something else.

Had Geraint not always been a mirror gone wrong? His reflection different from the face before my eyes. Yet did mirrors not signify challenge and change? How my instinct sensed that answers were close by. Clearly something potent from the past had entered the present. Had red energy aroused in Geraint the desire for conquest, struggle, battle? Enticed his emotions? Drawn him toward my being? Yet the white of intuition commanded my tongue to be silent. My eyes must wait and watch. The stronger the mystery, the surer his interest.

Clearly woodlands and water held secrets tempting his desires, testing my strength. A scent which Geraint had sensed. Were the passions of Ruby Red, the coolness of Diamond White, not forces already in play? No longer need I concern myself with reflections Geraint might be seeking. Now my mind prepared to explore the maze of my own dazzling mirrors. How my memory sought the many myriad scenes connected to my own past, present, future! Yes I, Aisling, was ready to welcome *whomever* and *whatever* came into my life.

There were no dragons to slay,
only his inner thoughts to conquer.

· XI ·
FACES OF
FATE

GERAINT WAS NERVOUS, HIS MOOD AGITAT-
ED. Nothing pleased him any more. Restless with
indecision, he resisted whatever change was com-
ing. He found himself out of control and out of sorts! His ruffled black hair had not
been cut in weeks. His bedroom, unattended, was in constant disarray. Discarded
clothing lay heaped on the corner chair. He refused to open any window. Anxious
habits had reappeared. Pacing up and down the stagnant bedroom, he muttered to
himself. Tension had brought shortness of breath. His behavior was abrupt. Fingers
constantly tapping, his left eye fluttered at unexpected moments. Not being *in command* had brought about depression.

Clearly his strategy had not succeeded. How Aisling had intruded on his mind,
her allure more powerful than anticipated. Her refusal had left something he wanted
to possess. Geraint now was obsessed in a most outrageous way. As she sauntered
down school corridors, his eyes would follow her. Her streaky hair irritated him.
Everything about her piqued his indignation. Some strange magnetism drew madness from his mind. So strong was this fascination that fears made him seek the opposite of his desires. In his anxiety he did everything possible to avoid Aisling.

Yet his anger compelled him to conquer her. Why then did his mind meander
with his moods? He found himself disappearing around corners, even trying to discover her plans. Her personality had become more powerful than his pride. His agitation was irrational. What thoughts did Aisling arouse that he could not remember?
Some intangible sensation so close—yet remote enough to seem beyond his reach.

Did ambivalence not attract *and* irritate his ego? Clearly the avoidance of his
advances had not been appreciated. Rejection by another destroyed the presence of
his power, refusal increased his determination. Her strange ways compelled him.
Impassioned, he turned towards his diamondback rattlesnake. Geraint found him-

61

self shouting, "Why don't you help me? I give you everything and get nothing in return!" Yet not once did his sleeping snake stir. Desperation seized his soul. "Wake up!" Geraint yelled again. "Why don't you heed me?" Vexed, he fell back upon his thoughts. How was he to grasp the knowledge Aisling held secret? His psyche needed her wisdom, wanted her irrational intuition.

Throwing his clothes on the floor, Geraint sank into his solitary chair. Tapping fingers reflected the uneasiness held within. Had he lost all sense of logic? Had his rational mind stopped functioning? What had happened to his energy and excitement? Geraint did not know how he had shifted from solitude to this game of conquest. Perhaps his willpower suddenly craved the surprise of seduction. Had his sexual fires been ignited? Had he become frustrated, not knowing what to do with their flames? Geraint considered this idea preposterous. No, this felt more like trials and temptations. Agitation mixed with arrogance.

Yet feelings of fire always made his warrior energy rise, arousing his need for combat and courage. Such strategy required a plan. Did Aisling's elusiveness not imply a strength behind her sudden changes? How often Geraint had watched her move from fear to precarious places. How many times had he seen her switch from the expected to the unexpected! Yet never could he fathom the thinking of her mind. Flighty and unclaspable, Aisling would dart in unanticipated directions. Did these evasive movements not awaken in him some need for strife, struggle, success? Was something mysterious attracting him towards her maddening ways?

As a tree remote and rooted, so Aisling appeared untouchable. She alone fathomed the deep untamed forests of her mind. Cool and calm, her reserved nature stayed aloof. No one interfered with the choices that she made. Yet Geraint wanted his own way. Never could he forget the birthday vow of many months ago. Would not the powers of prophecy and healing return to him? Yet this could happen only through a female voice. How he regretted what his pledge had brought about! His psyche had not prepared him for the aloofness of Aisling. Such ideals demanded head not heart, or so he thought.

Did Aisling with manners cool and collected, offer the charisma of charm? "No way!" he smirked, shaking his hair in disbelief. Her temperament was serious, not seductive. Yet some quixotic part of him longed for the beautiful maiden of his dreams. How he had deliberately avoided such a search. How the hero in his mind knew only of arduous tasks and menacing creatures to overcome! Never had his psyche sought a maiden from his heart. Life seemed a path that Fate had forced upon him. How Geraint thought himself a hero whom the Heavens would always command. Being destined, so his honor believed in destiny. Yet, accustomed to attracting attention to himself, his pride had never been thwarted by another.

Abruptly he rose from the chair, threw open the window. Perhaps fresh breezes would clear the cobwebs from his mind. Shaking his head, he scoffed, "So what if Aisling declined my advances? Why should doubts stop my determination?" Then Geraint stalked about the bedroom, "So what if Aisling knows things mystical and mysterious? Why should my desires not discover magical ways myself?" Then did he stop pacing. Suddenly Geraint stood before his sleeping snakes. "Why should her inner worlds enchant me? Why should I not battle for my beliefs? And what about her does my mind fancy, yet fear?"

His thoughts flowed with agitation. Yet still he dreaded the loss of control that came with intuition and instinct. Telepathic messages, that Aisling obviously had sent, shattered his psyche. Were such thoughts too forceful for him to fathom? How Geraint preferred pen and paper, then could his mind plot and plan. Mind games prevented his privacy from being protected. How he disliked that Aisling could *read* his thoughts and *see* beyond his strategy! She had found entrances into the deep and dark unconsciousness of his mind.

Yet was such an attraction not forcing him into action? Unforeseen, Geraint heard a hissing sound coming from his beloved snake. Was his diamondback rattlesnake not coiled upright, demanding his attention? Geraint looked into its piercing eyes! Yet, receiving only silence, so he sent several thoughts. Frequently would an answer enter Geraint's mind. Carefully did he phrase his words, "Should my constancy continue to chase Aisling?" No reply returned. Then did Geraint rub his cheeks. "Should this matter be dismissed?" Still no answer came. He ran his fingers through his messy hair. "Should another solution be sought?" Suddenly the snake hissed but a brief second. Geraint paced up and down the bedroom. What other direction might he possibly pursue? What else had disturbed his thoughts? Did anyone other than Aisling aggravate his mind?

Then, between the seconds of a breath, Geraint flashed on Vivienne. How he disliked her red gold hair and secretive sea green eyes. She incited his indignation, reawakened rage! Just seeing her at school made him surge with an imaginary gold sword. Something strange in him demanded justice. Righteous feelings would surface, emotions so absurd Geraint dared not relate them to reality. Yet never had they spoken. Not once had he seen her face to face. Then why did feelings of bewitchment run terror through his heart? How often had Geraint imagined her face reflected in a shining shield! Then swiftly would he sever her head with his sacred sword. Slowly would he watch two drops of blood fall upon the floor. Victorious and proud, the reward of a hero would be his.

Vivienne, whom he feared, was Aisling's only friend. Always her sea green eyes evoked this outrageous scene. How had such thoughts reached his mind? What paranoia possessed him? What rage thirsted for revenge? How Geraint hated when their heads huddled together, Vivienne whispering something secret to her friend.

Then would bizarre images bombard his mind. Sometimes he thought he was seeing the same female from a different point of view. Other times, his mind would blur Vivienne and Aisling together.

Yet Geraint felt frustrated. How he loathed being caught in the coming chaos! Some gnawing curiosity was driving him from his cloistered bedroom. Would cold water calm his fiery nerves? His bathroom mirror brought relief, at least his face looked sane. Might frenzied thoughts not come from the shadow of his soul? Perhaps a demon of the past possessed his psyche. Could such spirits harm a hero protected by sacred snakes? Geraint found himself shouting through the bathroom door. His diamondback rattlesnake suddenly sat alert. "Is Vivienne the one you mean?" he called. Loud hissing sounds rang throughout the bedroom, as the mirror nearby began to shake!

Yet such a reply did not please him. Already his life was complicated beyond control. And did not Aisling still intrigue him? No way would these feelings leave his mind. Was seeking Vivienne perhaps a vain attempt to cover damaged pride? There were no dragons to slay, only his inner thoughts to conquer. How his mind controlled all actions! At least solitude had given him a chance to think. Honoring his diamondback rattlesnake, Geraint now saw colors never seen before. His snake sparkled as a ruby gem, yet was clear as crystal light. "What do you offer to read into my mind?" came the telepathic thought behind its hissing sounds.

Geraint held his breath lest this precious moment cease. Then cautiously did he reply, "Behold, beloved snake, my clock of gold!" Slithering into his coils, the snake replied:

Perhaps you might consider something from your mind.
Power over possessions is no concern of mine.

Geraint, no longer disturbed by defeat, thought again. Carefully did he reply, "Oh, slippery snake, what part of my mind do you wish to take?" To which the snake seductively answered:

The part that fears the waters of the night.
The part that does not want to face its fright.

Geraint shut his eyes, hoping the scene might disappear. Instead, the diamondback rattlesnake flicked its poisonous tongue, led him to the highest rung. Had the moment of decision not come? The drama of victory or failure? His heart raced faster than his head! Was this not the demand Geraint so long had dreaded? "Oh, wisdom snake, my honor obeys your command," he solemnly said, "So shall

64

my services submit to your soul. My heart falls upon your fangs." Then did distressed Geraint await the decision. The venomous snake struck with strength:

> Listen to my plans!
> Heed my words with care!
>
> Vivienne, Lady of the Lake, knows your present dirge.
> Beneath her sea of sorrow must you quickly surge.
> What Fate awaits so shining mirrors tell.
> Then crystals shall reflect should all go well.

Suddenly did Geraint come to attention. "Oh, learned serpent, how may this deed be done?" he asked with trepidation. The reply was strange indeed:

> Through darkness comes the light.
> In light shines all things bright.
>
> Frozen are those who writhe in pain.
> Beings whom Geraint now must free again.

Geraint tried to interpret this image. Yet, as the snake retreated into himself, further words came forth:

> Wisdom trapped in anger
> Brings torture to the troubled mind.
> Only by following the pursuit of peace
> Might the sea of sorrow find release.
>
> So shall snakes observe you through the night
> Watching to *see* if Geraint finds his *sight*.

Then did the silence of the sun permeate the room. Rays of red cast shadows on his snakes, and sunshine lit the darkness of his mind. "Were my feelings perhaps wrong?" Geraint muttered to himself. "Maybe Vivienne is mystical after all." Then faintly could serpentine sounds be heard:

> Pursue her in haste!
> There is no time to waste!
> For now does she thirst!

With bursting energy Geraint prepared himself. Hastily dressing, he felt re-lieved that action had returned.

"Cut through illusion, Aisling.
Sever what does not serve your life."

· XII ·
SEA
SERPENTS

HOW MY SHADOW SELF SEETHED WITH SEC-
RETS! My mind went back in time rather than
soaring through space. The sensation haunted me,
my shadow always pulling me into the past, the unexpected and unexplained tan-
talizing my thoughts. How my psyche seemed suspended in silence! Hidden scenes
hovering in my shadow. The Kingdom under the Sea, silver serpents, magical mermaids, coral conch shells. Did they not seem a madness from my mind? Why should
spirits live in seas and ponds, lakes and rivers, under waterfalls, within whirlpools?
Why should anything exist under churning waters? Frozen beings in crystal palaces,
hidden in silver chambers. Passages and tunnels with untold views. From *where*,
and *why*, did such curious ideas arise?

Yet, whenever my mind wandered, these spaces felt familiar. Sometimes my
psyche seemed a silver mermaid, swimming through the sea, waiting upon the
shore. Other times was mad Medusa not *me*? And Vivienne. Was she not the mortal
psychic Queen Medusa? Yet why were her sisters immortal? Those frightening gorgon females, terrifying winged monsters with claws of brass, leathery scales, tusks
like boars, protruding tongues. What warnings came from their wisdom? How these
images bombarded my thoughts, became phantom pictures in my mind. Visions
which burst when others bothered me.

Through my shadow self these myths became alive. Had my psyche not
sympathized with Vivienne's mysterious ways? Was her charisma not cautious, yet
hovering on the edge of a cliff? Her sensitivity sliding into an abyss, slithering like a
serpent. Her sea green eyes drawing my mind to her thoughts, her psychic presence
seemed not in present time. Rather an ancient memory of anger toward men. Some
sense of desperation that destroyed. A frantic cry to claim her power place again, an
urgency to right what had been wrong.

How often had my Silver Dream shown me scenes beneath the turbulent sea. Yet now beauteous Vivienne, as mystical Queen Medusa, had transformed into an ugly hag. Her red gold hair was knotted as petrified snakes entwined, her serpentine curls spreading as fingers across the churning waters. How distraught was this drama in my dream! How disturbed were her demons! Wrath had replaced her arrogance. Her seduction turned to sadness, enchanting eyes a sea of sorrow. Yet bright ribbon reins were clutched within her hands. Where was mad Medusa furiously directing the winged horse Pegasus? Why was a wreath of white roses around her serpentine hair? And what had happened to her beauteous face? Now, so ghastly and grotesque, she seemed a drama of death itself.

Only rays of moonlight shone within this sea of sadness. Then did its waters separate, stormy waves permitting all to pass. Yet what was their determined destination? How my shadow self wanted to know! Suddenly Aisling of the dream demanded attention. My mind became spirited. Then did my voice urge angry Medusa and proud Pegasus to hasten with speed. Something peculiar had made my psyche anxious. "Where are you going?" my voice shouted through my sleep. Outraged Medusa replied, "How dare you disturb my darkness! No force has confronted my face for eternal years!" Yet my words were not wasted. My mind certain that, before the coming dawn, hideous Medusa must reach the Crystal Castle. Somehow her madness must awaken Queen Agan before her serpent eyes confront a tale untold. How my psyche wanted to protect Medusa's soul! "Take care!" my shadow self called through the stormy sea. "Remember the old woman with green hair and long green fangs called Jinni! Avoid her stagnant weed-covered waters, ensnaring those who dare to pass." Then did waves silence my words. Incensed Medusa, unwilling to heed my thoughts, turned away from me.

My dream self looked towards Pegasus instead. Majestic and magical, how he bolted through raging waters. His hoofs sped onwards through opposing tides. How often Aisling of the dream held her breath. Submerged by the sea itself, my dream body lost sight of him. Then my clarity returned. Yet had my mind been wrong? Was Pegasus not struggling to leave these seething waters? Indeed his mouth was frothing, his head bucking. Reaching for the stars he sought the Milky Way, the serpent pathway in the sky. Yet raging Medusa was pulling tighter on the ribbon reins. Had his rebellion excited her rage? Clearly anger had awakened anxiety.

Yet, no matter how swiftly they flew, other scenes appeared. Why, look! There was Captain Nodi, surging with strength, standing upon a sea of stars. Clad in glistening gold, his splendid golden palace rose from the sea. There, before its golden gates, awaited a golden chariot drawn by Tritons. Blowing crystal conch shells they were heralding Captain Nodi's arrival. Standing without a shadow had Captain Nodi not become Poseidon, Lord of the Sea? Was he not the King of the Waters,

Ruler of this Realm? At his command white stallions with golden manes would race through darkened waters. How furious and fearsome seemed their fate!

Yet how sullen and severe Captain Nodi had become. His voice now thundered through my ears, "Curses on those who severed her *sight*, who destroyed the mystical Queen Medusa of my dreams! So shall anger avenge those who did her harm. May floods fall upon fields, may rivers rise from constant rains. May majestic mountains plunge into the sea." Yet to whom was he speaking? His wrathful voice shaking the sea and sky. How my dream self watched Captain Nodi raise high his silver trident, above the crest of each new wave did he brave the storm.

Yet look! Was that not cantankerous Urag? Were his golden wings not carrying him far from Captain Nodi? Was the bird not reaching towards Heaven for help? His golden beak shone bright as the morning sun. Radiant with release, his energy soared with wondrous light. Had freedom not transformed his fears? Upwards did his golden wings spiral with inspiration. His mind had triumphed over matter! For behold, Urag had reached the rising sun and entered its heat without blinking an eye. Had he not transformed into a golden eagle? My dream self watched the beautiful bird burst as sunbeams of gold light, then quickly disappear.

Something warned my shadow self to take care. Had my psyche not found itself amidst conflicts of power and potency? Then did my mind accept a struggle of another sort. Suddenly my dream body appeared as a priestess of prophecy. Through ritual and rites were my words beseeching fierce Medusa, my energy attracting her attention. She must reach the Crystal Castle by dawn, before Heaven destroyed the Earth! How the priestess of prophecy pleaded for mad Medusa to consider the mysteries of mirrors and moving waters.

"Are you prepared to heed my help?" my shadow self shouted. The hag Medusa returned her gorgon stare. Dare my dream body penetrate the mystery behind this mask? Had her fierce eyes not turned many men to stone? Surely Medusa's mind permitted no intrusion. "You are petrified in an ancient pattern!" my shadow voice screamed through the perilous sea. Then did the priestess of prophecy speak once more. "The time has come for psychic Queen Medusa to be honored again. Dark rays of death must cease to claim these serpent curls. Her dreams of night must come to life again!" Yet indignant Medusa wanted to fight this battle alone. Then did Aisling of the dream implore once more, "Too many females are entangled in your ancient ways. Please help me save the sensitivity of your *sight*. May waters of emotions free your fears. May the sea cleanse your soul tonight. Take this crystal mirror within your wrathful hand, and deeply look within yourself."

Without awaiting a reply, my shadow self attached the silver mirror to a silver thread. Then did my dream self dangle the mirror before mad Medusa. How the object held a truth of its own. This mirrored image would reveal the shadow of

69

her soul. Then might seething Medusa *see* her spirit in its shining glass. Then would visions crystal clear appear upon moving waters. Yes, angry Medusa must honor her shadow, forgive and then forget. Yet would her wrath surrender to a mystic mirror that might offer her a miracle?

Suddenly my energy collapsed. Was the resistance of hideous Medusa stronger than my desires? Impulsively did my dream eyes look backwards. In that instant of doubt, everything dissolved. My mind was nowhere. Thoughts were forgotten. No shadow self watched from above. Instead, through the deep darkness, another scene appeared. Some strange sensation guided me towards the narrow boat Nebulae. Drifting through the boatman's cabin, suddenly Aisling of the dream was on its upper deck, my dream self sitting astride the white winged horse Pegasus. Had my psyche skipped a stone through time? My mind experienced release, my breathing deepened, my senses felt alive. With vibrant energy my thoughts encouraged proud Pegasus.

Suddenly my dream body swam forwards and entered the shadow of mad Medusa. Holding onto her waist, my tunnel *sight* peered through her ruby eyes. Coupled together, we swam through the turquoise sea, shadow to shadow, soul to soul. Petulant Pegasus ceased all resistance. His curiosity following the waves in motion, my dream body encouraging angry Medusa. "Tell me the truth! Declare your destination!" Finally mad Medusa replied, "My wrath seeks the Crystal Palace. There the golden sword of Chrysaor must be reclaimed." Faintly my mind recalled his name. Before my questioning eyes, visions of a shining gold sword appeared.

How we surged through this darkened sea! Yet, as enraged Medusa became more exuberant, Pegasus flew with foreboding. Still my mind remained perplexed. Once again did my tunnel eyes pierce the third eye of Medusa. As gazing into a crystal ball, a vivid scene appeared before my *sight*. There gleamed a Palace of Ice, glistening as frozen light! Yet this Crystal Castle, dazzling as a diamond night, was confined by crimson candles aflame with glows of red. Ferocious waves crashed but never reached these ruby flames. Then did my tunnel eyes behold the mystical Queen Medusa.

She was frozen upon a translucent throne of ice. Only her hair remained radiant red gold. Many silver snakes entwined around her arms, her frozen feet shrouded by magical mermaids. Their shining scales, turquoise blue and emerald green, protected her power with their radiant rays. Yet the warmth of these jewels dared not penetrate the frozen Queen. Immortal silver snakes sat before the entrance of this frosty tomb, their forked tongues ready to strike whomever threatened their treasure. How the power of their poison protected this sanctuary of peace. Yet might this be a shrine within the sea itself, where rites and rituals had once been performed? A sacred site recalling the temple where psychic Queen Medusa had been cursed.

Where was mad Medusa furiously directing the
winged horse Pegasus?

Yet my shadow self was torn by tension and turmoil. So many temptations and trials had tumbled through torrential waves. Were ancient myths not turning on themselves? How my determined voice now shouted from strength! "Wrathful Medusa's rage must be released!" Then did my courageous mind call out, "Victory to mad Medusa! Don't let anyone stop you now!" Poor Pegasus reared, worried about himself. Yet might not the brothers, Pegasus and Chrysaor, reclaim their rights again? A touch of Medusa's madness encouraged my surging strength. Was Aisling of the dream not shouting through this sea of sadness? Swinging her arms about, holding a golden sword in her hand.

Then was the voice of Vivienne heard through my dreams. "Cut through illusion, Aisling! Sever what does not serve your life!" My startled shadow self called back, "Where are you speaking from?" Then did the smiling voice of Vivienne sound again. "Right before you, silly." How had I forgotten? Were not the mortal Queen and mad Medusa meshed together in my mind? "Look at your raised right hand," Vivienne returned my thought. Was my arm not waving an empty red sheath? Yet what had happened to the golden sword within? Surely objects do not appear and disappear at will.

Once again my tunnel eyes peered into wrathful Medusa's mind, and my psyche discovered a darkened dungeon. In a chamber beneath frozen Queen Medusa blazed the shining sword of Chrysaor. Its glistening gold was aflame with raging fire, its sharpened blade frozen in a granite rock. Yet nothing more could Aisling of the dream ascertain. My physical body, asleep in the four-poster bed, had seen all it wished to *see*. A sheet of blankness covered my eyes. "It's all right, Aisling!" exclaimed the voice of Vivienne. "Come home. You have watched enough for now!" Then was her distant voice drowned by thunderous waves.

My physical body awakened with questions flying through my mind. Why was the red sheath without its golden sword? Why had my right hand raised its phantom blade above my head? Was this not the shadow of Chrysaor's sword? The sword which indignant Medusa had sworn to hold within her conquering hands. Yet had I, Aisling of the dream, not become as mad as Medusa herself? At once my determined mind decided to telephone Vivienne. My psyche needed to know if she as well had dreamt this dream within a dream.

The Moon lighted these crystal clear waters,
as her reflection danced and spun upon itself.

· XIII ·
NIGHT
SCHOOL

IT WAS DUSK, AND VIVIENNE HAD BEEN SITTING before her dressing table mirror for what seemed hours. She had been thinking about her appearance. Had the pearl grey sweater and blue harem trousers not been perfect for the portrait sitting? The face cream had made her skin more porcelain white, the pale shadow, upon her lids, had turned her eyes more blue than green. To be attractive in a seductive way intrigued her. How the tension of *look but do not touch* brought sensual reactions from another. She had relished beguiling the portrait painter. Her bewitching silence stimulated the atmosphere. Had her psychic waves not titillated his studio? "How about staying for dinner?" he nonchalantly proposed, "Fresh linens on the bed!" Vivienne demurely reminded him of her chaste status, something she had no inclination to change. On leaving the studio she had swung her hips several times just to emphasize the point.

Night-time was when she brooded. Seated before the dressing table mirror, her conduct now seemed questionable. Nothing seemed to satisfy the fantasy of her imagination. Only the drama of indecision delighted her. Yes, the painter had made Vivienne feel noticed, although few words passed between them. They always spoke mind to mind, dancing in the web of thoughts. Yet now she wondered about his reactions. Had he observed her turquoise bracelets, entwined around her arms? Her new pearl grey sweater, loose but softly curved upon her blossomed form? Both had been birthday presents. On that special day the painter had given her one perfect red rose. A cliché she returned with a secret smile.

The portrait sitting had been thrilling but thwarting. Now her mind felt erratic. Vivienne slowly cleansed her skin. The tiredness after such tension always left her face depressed. Why did her emotions bounce between delight and despair? Why was she so dissatisfied with life? She could not imagine *what* her psyche was seek-

73

ing. Shrugging her shoulders, she pulled her father's cast off nightshirt from the dresser drawer and slipped into it. Then, tucking herself into bed, she switched off the bedside lamp.

The next morning Vivienne awoke with a start. She neither believed *where* her body had been during the night, nor *what* her eyes had seen. Had she suffered a nightmare or an ecstatic experience? Her dream had been more than disturbing. Jewelled visions sparkled with purple peacocks, flashing diamond stars, luminescent red lights. Images which had lured her psyche through bizarre spaces. Still half asleep, her dream memory floated above the night covers, her dream mind drifting around the bedroom. Feeling incredibly light, a strange sense of exhilaration warmed her body beneath the covers.

Yet Vivienne could hardly comprehend *how* this escapade had occurred. Without switching on the bedside lamp, she scribbled in the dark. Everything her mind could remember was scrawled on a note pad. Her fingers would not stop as Vivienne wrote down every scene that had passed before her closed eyes. Yet the dream unfolded backwards. Was she not watching a movie in reverse? Her ears still heard voices from the dream, each spoken word was recalled. Every detail from the night journey reappeared, the vibrant lights, sparkling images, dazzling scenes. Yet how had such fantastic visions entered her mind?

Yes, she remembered going to bed disturbed. In the silence of the bedroom she had reviewed the day, accepting its hidden anguish. Playing with fire had created this restless state. Its sensual tensions were familiar. Before sleeping she considered the consequences of her choices. Her psyche, conscious of other possibilities, was ready for change. With such feelings, Vivienne had closed her tired eyes. Resting on her back, toes touching, hands upon her stomach, she had fallen into a deep sleep. She remembered drifting into spaces of peace. Her breathing became quiet, worrisome thoughts released themselves. Disturbances from the day dissolved. So she had slipped into the silence of her mind. The night screen before her eyes turned to velvet black, then tiny specks of sparkling light attracted her attention. Vivienne watched them expand into rays of crimson. Silver and gold keys appeared, waiting to be turned. Her curiosity had chosen the brightest one, and from that moment onward the dream became outlandish.

Even thinking about the night voyage made her heart tremble. What a frightening sensation of being suspended in space! Had her dream body not separated from her physical body? Vivienne had stood outside of herself. There had been neither darkness nor shadows, only forms emerging from light, then slipping from *sight*. Feelings of amazement and confusion, even terror, had shaken her beyond reality. Then had Vivienne floated from space to space, drifting in a soft, strange energy. Vaguely she recalled incredible lights that glowed red and white. Tones heating in intensity, then bursting into brightness. Had they not become beacons of blinding light?

Barely realizing *where* she was, Vivienne had entered a Silver Bubble. White light blazed from all directions. Silver sparkles had dazzled her dream eyes! Then, suddenly, the light dissolved and bizarre beings appeared, diaphanous figures drifted around, faces foreign yet familiar. Transparent beings floating through the crystal sphere.

Then silence bathed the Silver Bubble. As seats unfolded from its crystal walls, these curious figures found their places. Vivienne, sitting to the left of its crescent shape, hardly recognized herself. She was draped in silks of black and gold, her ravishing red gold hair floating in space. Metallic silver snakes curled around her arms. A radiant red ruby shimmered between her sea green eyes. The full moon glittered as a garland upon her head. Hands held sweet fruits and ripe grains. She glowed with the season of Summer, scented with musk and patchouli, her vibrations reflecting the warmth of life.

Vivienne searched the Silver Bubble to *see* whom else had come aboard. Why, there was Aisling, totally transparent, poised in the center of this semi-circle. Draped in diaphanous white, the crescent moon beamed as a diamond wreath upon her flowing hair. How virgin pure and self-assured she looked, her smile one of enchantment. How her innocence attracted everyone to her sparkling beauty. Yet Vivienne's eyes were drawn towards her feet. Her shoes were of silver glass, each slipper shining from the light of the moon. Then Vivienne stared at her hands, emblazoned with the sign of the huntress, the crescent horn of the moon brimming with crimson blood.

And look who sat to the right of Aisling! None other than Geraint, the mythic hero come to life. His right hand held a golden sword, his left a mirror shield. Diamondback rattlesnakes coiled around his waist. His bare chest was covered by a cloak of dashing red, embroidered with glistening gold. His red tunic radiated with vibrant rays of the sun. His sandals were shining glass of gold. They seemed to fly his soul to Heaven and return his body to Earth.

Intuitively did her dream eyes look to the left. Seated besides Vivienne was an ancient hag with skin of granite grey! What once was beauteous hair had turned to writhing snakes, sea green eyes were beads of ruby red. Clutched in her right hand was a golden sword, her left hand clenched the reins of a white winged horse. Yet, how Vivienne resembled this ugly hag! Both wore ravishing silk of black and gold, and each had arms entwined with silver snakes. Only the moon above their heads was not the same, the waning moon reflected the wisdom of the hideous hag. Yet its luminescent glow had begun to fade from sight. How Vivienne worshipped the full moon! For a brief moment they acknowledged one another. Then Vivienne's right hand took the golden sword, but never would the old crone release the reins of the white winged horse. Instead she turned and said, "Remember things that were, things that are, things that yet may be."

Quickly Vivienne looked away. Desperately her eyes searched the Silver Bubble for relief. Then did her dream self espy the Serpent Queen Agan. Elegant in spiral form, the mysterious Queen glistened with emerald and turquoise jewels. No one in the crystal sphere escaped her gaze! Each phase of the moon rested within her meditative hands. Her intuition protected the wisdom of oceans and seas, lakes and ponds, rivers and streams. Did her depth not reflect the silence of still waters, her serene smile protecting the secrets of life? Yet rays of the scorching sun now disturbed her dreams. How Vivienne empathized with this psychic Queen, her intuition certain that some furious force had once torn them asunder. Their connection briefly burst in her mind. Then did their eyes acknowledge one another.

Some magnetic current pulled her mind from the Serpent Queen towards the center of the Silver Bubble. Suddenly, within its crescent shape, a dazzling screen unrolled. Standing besides this silver screen stood two exotic crystal forms. Poised on the left was Diamond White, on the right was Ruby Red. Vivienne had never seen anything like them before. Only Aisling of the dream applauded their appearance, beaming in recognition of their return. Streaming from their crystal fingers were rays of shining light. Brilliant white and red beams pointing to the silver screen. "Welcome to Night School!" they both exclaimed with delight.

Then Diamond White stepped forward, crystal arms waving as sparkling wands. The shimmering screen became a magic mirror. "Tonight we shall celebrate the crescent moon!" she exclaimed with pleasure. Ruby Red replied, "Perhaps another night shall be the Knight of Swords." To this Diamond White paid no heed. "Reach up with your left hand," she then instructed. "Now hold the horn of the waxing, crescent moon. How this new silvery moon enhances inspiration, enchantment, imagination. Is it not the mystery of the feminine world as yet unrevealed?" Once again the Silver Bubble burst with blinding white light. Only the vision on the mirror screen remained. From that moment onwards Vivienne was spellbound. Mesmerized, she watched Diamond White encircle her crystal arms, spinning them faster and faster. Then, in the instant of a breath, Diamond White was transformed into a youthful maiden dressed in transparent white. A crescent moon of diamonds sparkled as her crown. Her skin scented with the sweetness of jasmine, the spice of myrtle. White rose and musk emanated from her aura. "The crescent moon is youth!" beamed this glowing maiden. What marvels did Vivienne then behold! The mirror flowed with scenes of crystal streams and wishing wells, fountains of youth and gushing waterfalls. There were flower buds on every woodland tree, birds chirping songs of Spring. "So began the beginning of time, when all was hopeful and energy high. When endless choices danced through the forest, and one cared only about oneself."

The graceful maiden then stepped into the mirror screen. Standing above the horizon, she beckoned forth the crescent moon, summoning its silver light. "How

76

my heart yearns for a mirror pond flowing from underground springs. Water without tributaries or outlets. Waters as warm as Spring itself. Waters which do not freeze in Winter, and are not chilled by the dark of the Night." Uttering these words, the youthful maiden was drawn deep into a woodland scene. Vibrant trees of silver birch and silver fir enchanted the forest of her mind. As she raced with energy wild, the maiden darted through the thicket. Trees quivered. The earth trembled with the marvel of a miracle.

Were her roots not hidden beneath these trees? Were her arms not open to the winds? Was she not a spirit of nature? The maiden breathed the sweet fragrance of birth itself. Her newfound movements, unpredictable and flighty, protected this sacred space. None dared violate these virgin ways. Did she not reflect the crescent moon, the brilliance of diamond rays? How her fierceness belonged to herself alone! With wildness did she claim what was hers to maintain. Untamed as nature, so she wandered through woodlands and waters, her movements intuitive and impulsive.

"How my heart is the first dream!" she had called to the crescent moon. "My hair blows in winds of change, my eyes search for pools of magical mineral waters! Hidden are answers to my questions. Upon still waters do my wishes reflect themselves." Then, in silence, did the maiden dance upon the crescent moon. Yet only this moon could reveal the many secrets which she held within. "Am I not protected from worries of the world?" she asked in truth. Impatient and rebellious, formless and free, how many strange ways she did not understand!

Vivienne, enchanted, watched the maiden find her secret lake. The moon lighted these crystal clear waters, as her reflection danced and spun upon itself. Objects within soon changed to silver threads. Here the maiden sought secrets shown to *sight*. Yet mirror reflections revealed her past patterns not resolved. Slowly did the maiden pull silver threads from these waters of emotions. Then did answers arise from the depths of the secret lake. Yet none of this could Vivienne *see*. She witnessed only the maiden born anew. Through shadows in the sea, she emerged from the forest of the night, into reflections of the silver moon.

Then did these silver threads from the sea mesh into silver shadows of the night. As visions and voices melted into one, so the maiden became Diamond White again. The mirror screen began to fade away. Vivienne, floating back from sleep, heard the crescent moon call once more, "Where is the maiden who yields to all, yet is penetrated by none?" Once again did Aisling of the dream appear in translucent white, scented with jasmine and musk. Then did Vivienne wonder, "Could this maiden in the silver mirror have been my curious friend?"

Now, nearly awake, Vivienne shook her sleepy head. She clutched her feather pillow, lest her mind fall back into this dream of dreams and she lose her way again.

Yet *Geraint could have been invisible, the mysterious mermaid*
paid him no heed.

*She was still tending her sea green hair
with her golden comb.*

· XIV ·

MERMAID MAGIC

DON'T PLAY WITH FIRE if you don't want to get burned." Well, no longer was Geraint disturbed by rejection. Aisling was not going to hinder his plans. With the strength of the sun behind him only brightness lay ahead. His preparations were near completion. Still, part of his birthday vow remained unfulfilled. Who was the female oracle in his pursuit of prophecy and healing? Surely he had erred to think Aisling *the one*. All tests came in three so certainly Geraint had failed the first. Perhaps his second chance was Vivienne, the elusive one with the sea green eyes and red gold hair.

The weekend came as a relief. Sunday was sacred to the family. Saturday secure for Geraint's personal plans. The next twenty-four hours were his alone. Then why did he feel so ambivalent? More rational than intuitive, his mind still needed to assess the situation. Structure and logic made him feel secure, never did Geraint trust his instinct. Only strategy brought success. Indecisive, he shrugged his shoulders. How perturbed he felt that plans plotted had gone awry! Yet he was determined that Aisling's dismissal was not going to disturb him. Then why was he still thinking about her? Surely his confidence and control had returned. His morning plans seemed clean and clear. After today he would concentrate on Vivienne and her vanity.

Saturday was dedicated to finding herbal plants for his healing experiments. His specific list could only be found in the forest. Rosemary, a woody divided root, would assist memory, quicken the senses, sharpen *sight*. Lavender stopped all passions of the heart. Thyme would clear all headaches. Fennel seeds, which cleansed the blood, could help to cure a serpent bite. Next Geraint planned to crush the leaves, their essences blended for healing oils. Then would the experiments in his bedroom begin.

Geraint busied himself in the kitchen, a silent and sacred place before dawn.

Softly humming he made a giant sandwich of brown bread, cheese, bean sprouts, to-matoes. Then a second one of cucumbers and tuna. In the larder he found an apple and an orange. The refrigerator yielded carrots and celery, and grape juice for his flask. Lastly did Geraint set aside honey for his snakes. This day would be without their protection. With guidebook in hand, knapsack on his shoulders, he prepared to leave for the forest. Softly closing the garden door, he slipped into daybreak.

Yet the morning mist veiled his sight. His compass could not find the in-tended path. As the forest grew deeper, Geraint passed trees of oak, beech, and cedar. In his diary of the day he wrote their size and location. On the higher ridge he hoped to find trees of acacia and ash. Near them would grow his herbs. Vaguely did Geraint recall one mysterious glen with musk rose and jasmine. Sure that his map was right, he was confused *where* his sense of direction proved wrong. Geraint found himself upon knotted roots of ancient pines growing in sparse soil. Yet *why* had he been un-able to follow his charted plan?

Having changed his course, however, did not alter his determination. Recheck-ing his compass, Geraint realized the error of his mind. Now was he within proximity of the pond. Again, taking his notebook, he wrote the details of his trip. He planned to leave the forest another way than entered. Yet what had happened? How had confu-sion consumed his mind? Surely thinking about females had begun the morning wrong. Exasperated, Geraint studied his waterproof watch. More than two hours had passed since leaving home. Rays of light now diffused the morning mist. Soft sun-shine covered the ground, and the air smelled sweet as wine scented with cinnamon.

Yet distances seemed longer than memory recalled. Feeling uneasy, once again did Geraint wonder *why* his plans had gone awry. Yet again his memory had erred. Had the pond not stretched in length, broadened in width? Suddenly shadows of willow and silver birch moved upon still waters, yet no breezes were about. Birds the color of writing, all black and white, hovered above the pond. Again, Geraint noted these details in his diary, lest his imagination play more tricks. Then he wrote the weather and temperature, hour of the clock, his present position. Deep in con-centration, unexpected sounds disturbed his thoughts. Was something slithering in the grass? Thinking this might be a snake for his collection, Geraint searched the water's edge. So doing he chanced to look into the quivering pond. There appeared a willowy shape, slowly rising to the surface. Gracefully swimming through deep waters, how this creature changed its form. Geraint thought aloud, "Perhaps what resembles a fair sized fish might be a shimmering serpent." Abruptly did its tail swiftly turn upon itself.

What had been calm turned into turbulent waters. What had been indistinct became bright as day. Had too many hours passed without him observing his watch? Strong sunlight now streamed upon the ground. Once again his sense of security was lost. Geraint, alert upon the grass, was bewildered and perplexed. This *loss of mind* never had happened before. "Wake up!" he shouted to himself, "Enough of this is enough!"

Then, for what seemed a short second, he peered into the deep waters. Strands of seaweed were caught around the serpent's head, green waves floating about this metallic fish. Geraint thought to observe for just another moment. Suddenly, darting from these waters, sprang not a silver serpent but a beauteous mermaid.

Geraint could have been invisible, for the mysterious mermaid paid him no heed. Gracefully she slid onto the grass and turned her side to him. How her bluish skin flustered him more than the beauty of her breasts. Then her sea green hair, flowing to her waist, mesmerized his mind. Elegantly did the mermaid sit erect, gaze into a silver mirror, tend her swirling hair with a golden comb. These beloved objects were placed in a precious pouch below her waist. Geraint noted that, although of gold, this comb folded as softly as fabric. Also, although daylight, the silver mirror reflected the crescent moon. He thought to write this data in his diary. Nowhere could his notebook be found. Exasperated, his attention abruptly returned to the enigmatic mermaid. She was still tending her sea green hair with her golden comb. Only now, when her turquoise eyes gazed into the silvered glass, she was scrutinizing his every movement.

Geraint was perplexed. Still, he was more embarrassed by the beauty of her body. "Why don't you return below the waters?" he declared, "You are decidedly disturbing my day." The mermaid tilted her head and continued combing her sea green hair with her golden comb. Coyly did she reply, "Then why did you beckon me forth?" Geraint shook his head in fierce denial. Vehemently did he respond, "No way did I call you! Why should I want anything from you?" She retorted without turning her head. "Did you not pray for a healing guide?" To this Geraint sharply replied, "The guide requested was not a naked mermaid." Yet the mermaid answered his thoughts which said, "Perhaps you are!" Thus she piquantly smiled. "Oh heavenly hero, come visit my house of coral conch shells floating beneath green seaweed waters!"

Teased by this temptress, Geraint's rational mind became decidedly desperate. Quickly he recalled every myth about mermaids. How they captured your soul, enchanted you to marry them, and lured you to secret palaces beneath the sea. His anxious heart throbbed, his panicked thoughts would not cease! A person without a soul belonged to no known world. Never could one ask *where* she disappeared each week, nor could her name be mentioned. Geraint, terrified, knew none of this made sense. Besides he had no intention of falling in love with anyone, and certainly not an enchanting naked mermaid luring him into the depths of the sea.

Upon hearing his thoughts the mermaid laughed. Then did waters of the pond quietly ripple. "Yet you are in love!" she declared. "Never! Never! Never!" Geraint defensively replied. "No," she giggled, "not with me." Then the mermaid teased. "Why you love many things! Your power and pride. Your sun and its strength. Your sanity and snakes. Your mind and its mercy. Your passion and pain. Your intensity and inspiration. Your wolves and women. Need my lips utter others things?" "Stop! Stop! Stop!" shouted Geraint, "You have said enough! What, mercurial mermaid, could you possibly want of me?" To which her beguiling eyes replied, "Why, hero of the sun, the serpent Queen Agan bids you forth. She is the beloved one beneath all lakes and seas and oceans. Her wisdom may guide you to heal and help and never harm!"

"Impossible!" Geraint thought, "That the guide to my heart lives in waters where one dares not swim. What nonsense can this be? Oh, shimmering serpent do you think me an absolute fool?" Convinced this creature heard not these words, he skeptically replied. "What, mysterious mermaid, pleases your Serpent Queen?" To which she coyly returned a suspicious smile. "Oh, heavenly hero, *that* you must learn for yourself." Once again in stillness did she stare at Geraint. Then, as speaking to herself, the mermaid murmured, "Ah, sadly my seaweed hair grows dry. Alas, the sun burns too strongly on my strands." So saying, she started to slip away. Impulsively did Geraint reach to touch her scales. Some fleeting temptation wanted to know if she was *real*. In that instant of approach, the mermaid slid her silver mirror into his trembling hands. Before Geraint could return this shimmering token, hastily did she disappear beneath the waters.

The magic silver mirror shook within his quivering hands! How could he turn away? Geraint now became curious. "Would looking within, just once, turn me to petrified stone?" The myths of mirrors and Medusa were all the same to him. Then Geraint decided to take a fleeting glance. No more, no less. The mirror, however, refused to reflect. Instead, his attention fell upon a hissing sound arising from beneath the pond. Clearly Geraint heard a siren call. "Listen well!" the voice exclaimed, "Queen Agan commands your snakes, their charms and harms, their poisonous tongues which heal. Now you must esteem this Serpent Queen, or never shall you meet your Eagle King!" The silver mirror throbbed within his hands. Its strong pulsations pulled Geraint to a place he resisted with all his might.

How he felt primordial chaos! Imprisoned beneath the sea, Geraint feared its waters would extinguish his fiery strength. The current pushed him past strange creatures of the sea, fish with waiting swords examined him with fierceness. Sea monsters almost devoured his frightened self. Geraint tumbled through coral reefs and seaweed waters. Tossed by ferocious tides, he surrendered to exhaustion. Then did he *see* the Kingdom under the Sea. It was surrounded by glass walls of lime green color. Yet no entrance was within sight. A phosphorescent bluish light covered its

82

Crystal Palace, the shower of moondust creating an illusion of life. When Geraint succumbed to its vibrations, he entered within. Never did he think that to depart would not be as easy.

And what did his eyes behold? A majestic mermaid crowned with a hood of cobra snakes. The serpent Queen Agan whose silver tail coiled beneath her waist, whose shimmering scales glistened as silver armor. Yet was she not armed for conflict? How her glimmering surface dazzled his astonished eyes! There was lapis lazuli, emerald gems and turquoise stones, diamonds brighter than stars. Silver and crystal wings spread across her back. Yet Geraint dared not glance at her necklaces of perfect turquoise beads, falling across the bareness of her breast.

How the Serpent Queen guarded her greeting, acknowledged his arrival. "My Kingdom was conceived when a sunbeam struck a snake," she forthright announced. To this Geraint flashed bright rays of the sun. "Well done!" Queen Agan applauded in approval, "So you have not forgotten from whence you came. Then surely you must wonder *why* my waters beckon you." Without awaiting a reply, she continued undaunted, "Such strange times demand subtle powers to unite. So your ancient strengths have been called upon." Hearing these words of destiny, Geraint responded with the bravery of the blessed. "Pray, honored Queen Agan, what may be the meaning of your words?"

The Serpent Queen scrutinized his eyes. "Heavenly hero recall the twelfth hour of the twelfth month of your birthdate this year," she decreed, "Then did you pledge to amend the wrongs once done. In times past did you not slay the female Python? The serpent whose dream oracles came from the womb of my earth. She who had been guardian of my Kingdom. The sacred serpent who protected my maidens. Their intuition! Their prophecies! Their omens!" Geraint shook with fright. Was this not the dreaded terror of the night? Yet Queen Agan grew stronger as she spoke, "Within a Crystal Castle beneath the silver sea is captured this treasure of *sight*. Now must you reclaim her powers, wisdom, earthly bliss. Such be the future of my thoughts."

Shocked, Geraint bowed his head. Too much was known about his deeds. Still the Serpent Queen was to strike her poisonous point. With anger did she release her ancient rage. "How dare you gather sacred snakes without offering homage to their sacred Queen!" Bombarded by their hissing sounds, Geraint awaited their striking at will. Again did he surrender to her silver sea. Accepting this respect, the Serpent Queen touched his lowered head. "Listen well, son of my soul," she said, "Queen Agan now tells a tale." Purposely did she pause for a slight second. Geraint held his anxious breath. "There lies a lost lake which is the window of the world," she spoke in measured words, "This lost lake anchors the sea and ocean, holding all in place. Long ago, these waters moistened the earth, nourished life itself. Now this lake of lament imprisons the sister of my soul. Captured in its Crystal Castle, she remains there petrified as stone, frozen as ice."

Geraint did not want to hear another word. Yet Queen Agan became more adamant. "In this Crystal Castle all beings are blind. They have forgotten many things. No longer can they *see* the light of the moon, the rays of the sun." She paused, awaiting an auspicious moment to rise. Instead, Geraint, hero of the sun, addressed her anguished voice. "Oh, esteemed one, how may my presence right these wrongs?" Then did his sun shine upon her darkened waters. Queen Agan sighed with sorrow. "Perhaps too many years have spun around themselves. Purple spider webs completely cover the sister of my soul. Only a human heart can tear these threads apart."

Her sadness seeped through his spirit. "I, Geraint, pledge to atone my ways," were his very words. Relieved, the Serpent Queen replied, "Only you can enter this Crystal Castle. Take care, son of my soul! Heated fountains spout ruby wine scented with the sweet aroma of cinnamon that makes one sleep. Tubs which contain pure water and hot dew await your arrival. You must cleanse yourself in the first, arise in the second. Take caution! This Castle, bathed in twilight, has never seen the rising sun. Only such rays of light can bring my sister back to life." Geraint took three steps backwards. Yet, as he slipped away from the sea, he clearly heard Queen Agan again:

Take Her from the Night!
Return Her to the Day!

So sings the siren of my soul!

With the sun warming his back, Geraint found himself high upon the hills. Why, he was within the glen where lay the herbs he sought. Yet, this very morning, had he not been before the pond? Clearly he had written details in his diary. Yet, taking out his notebook, all the pages were as blank as his mind. Without thinking, Geraint sketched drawings of the plants he had found. He noted their shapes and colors, the texture of the soil, heights to which each herb had grown. Then he abruptly stopped. What tricks were his thoughts playing? Had his mind not faded in and faded out again? How had he come upon this place? Why was he collecting herbs which could cure someone petrified to stone and frozen to ice? Shaking his head and shrugging his shoulders, his memory faded. Unable to answer his own questions, Geraint methodically continued his search for plants. After all, should he not be content? Had he not discovered the treasure which he sought?

At the mention of that word, Geraint's head began to buzz again. What *treasure* was he thinking about? Yet nothing more could he remember. Exhausted, he fell upon the grass, as the sun shone upon his tired eyes.

Then would my sixth sense
also see *strange persons,*
remote landscapes, bizarre scenes.

· XV ·
THE
SEARCH

THE SCHOOL LIBRARY WAS WHERE I, AISLING, WENT NEXT. A sense of urgency made me search for books about the sixth sense. Father's library held nothing about dreams and intuition. My eyes scanned every index. How quickly papers filled with notes that expanded my mind. Yet not one book answered my questions. Only unfamiliar phrases attracted my attention. Words like telepathy, clairvoyance, clairaudience, lucid dreams, and out of body explained some of my bizarre encounters.

Through telepathy, thoughts, emotions, and sensations were transmitted from one mind to another. Clearly my shyness always chose telepathic messages instead of confrontation. How often had my feelings answered a schoolmate by sending unspoken thoughts. Silent conversations which eased my embarrassment. Whether near or far away, their reaction always told me if such thoughts had been received. Yet was telepathy not a two way current? Schoolmates could send me messages, as my mind contacted them. Then would I, Aisling, be the receiver instead of the sender. Such vibrations moved as wave lengths through the air. Telepathic thoughts were constantly being transmitted, wave lengths never ceased. Human beings were always thinking of one another. The energy changed only when one person purposely sent a message to another. Then was the thought current directed with an answer in mind.

Were telepathic dreams not the same energy, except they happened during sleep? Clearly thoughts and emotions from my dream were conveyed to another in their dream. Would this not explain Geraint and Vivienne appearing in my visions? No doubt I, Aisling, had been in their dreams as well. Something ancient linked us on the psychic level. Yet no one spoke of this in reality. And what of the other strange beings in my Silver Dreams? Could they not be extensions of these telepathic wave lengths? Were all thoughts within time and space not connected? All

85

beings in the universal mind frame contacting one another. Might this explain what Night School dreams were all about?

Yet pictures were also transmitted through vibrations and wave lengths, visions sent and received. Library books described this as clairvoyance. That this sixth sense of sight could *see* things taking place somewhere else. Spontaneous pictures of specific events flashing in past, present, even future time. Yet, no matter the time frame, these happenings always *felt* in present time. Clairvoyance breaking through barriers of time and space. How the sixth sense felt beyond the wisdom of myself. Was this because its existence was so often denied? How often my clairvoyant mind felt suspended in space, limitless in potential, while everyday thoughts seemed restricted by the clock, confined by meetings and obligations.

Were childhood visions, dismissed as fantasy, not clairvoyant scenes from collective thoughts? Images belonging to the world of dreams, not classmate conversation? How these pictures came unbidden. Never could they be directed or controlled. They happened spontaneously, when awake or asleep. Then would my sixth sense also *see* strange persons, remote landscapes, bizarre scenes. How tingling sensations filled my body. Always my mind was astonished, wondering from *where* such peculiar pictures arose. Crystal clear scenes would appear before my open eyes. Visions so vivid their presence could not be denied. How their memory haunted my mind. Transparent scenes etched with crystal clarity. Yet never could my psyche fathom *what* had brought them before my sight.

And there were voices and sounds which my five senses could not hear. Sentences which seemed millions of miles away. Never did I, Aisling, know *why* or *when* such words were heard. Always they made me aware something special would occur soon. These voices arrived from nowhere, their ringing sounds disturbing my ears. High vibrations only animals could hear. Sometimes trumpets would call, sentences were spoken, even celestial symphonies with casts of thousands. Yet, when this music was heard the following day in school, my feelings felt frantic! Conversations were the same. During night sleep my dream self would hear them. Then how I panicked when they were repeated at school recess. Only library books now calmed my mind, describing this sixth sense as clairaudience.

Clearly flying dreams came from the sixth sense. Relaxed before slumber, my sleep body would slip from my physical body. Then, in twilight time, my dream self would hover on the ceiling, wander out bedroom windows, drift through doors. Standing straight with feet above the ground, often I glided past scenes never seen before. Floating on my back, sometimes swimming, how this transparent self moved horizontally through the air. At other times this dream body flew with wings, rising vertically upwards. I, Aisling, travelling out of my body, above trees and houses. Floating swiftly through wide spaces, backwards or upwards, how this second body moved at great speed.

Yet, after flying or floating for several nights, then would a lucid dream appear. Not unlike my waking life, the physical world stayed the same. Feeling light and loose, how familiar were places and faces. Dream landscapes could easily be recognized. Persons, known or unknown, were portrayed. Nothing changed identity as the dream proceeded, yet something special happened. An occurrence beyond the physical realm. Personality traits appeared that were hidden in reality, qualities denied in the day. How my mind followed these changes! How my second body understood that these were future thoughts. Then could my intuition predict *what* would happen.

Always, lucid dreams were crystal clear. My mind conscious of existing in an altered state. Yet, how my psyche wondered, "Am I, Aisling, dreaming? Watching myself dream? Has this dream been dreamt before? And now am I dreaming it again?" How this sixth sense blurred my other five senses. Yet might they be two different dimensions in parallel time? Such anxiety abruptly ended these lucid dreams. Then would my fear of falling bring everything to a sudden halt. Should my dream voice scream, "Where am I? Get me out of here!" then instantly everything dissolved. Fear created conflict! Emotional turmoil terminated such dreams of the night, as some unknown power pulled me backwards. With terrible sounds in my psyche, so everything came to a shocking halt. Awakened with a start, terror filled my heart. Only when my mind remained detached could lucid dreams stay crystal clear.

Yet other dreams were beyond flying above the physical world. Always, resting on my back before sleeping, my physical body would sink into myself. Conscious some separation was coming, my mind would submerge into water, into deep slumber. Sometimes my psyche seemed to turn into myself. Then the memory of another direction would begin. Deep dreams with long tunnels, winding stairs waiting to be climbed, corridors with endless courtyards. Through these passageways did my dream body proceed. Yet never was there a hint of length or location. What courage was required in these strange surroundings. Everything evaporated should my dream eyes look backwards. Only by remaining detached did these visions expand.

So different from lucid dreams, these passageways were beyond clocks and watches. Tunnels with bright lights at the end drew me into spirals. How my dream self spun in counterclockwise motions, everything turning into itself. Here my shadow split into multiple dream bodies. Here many mirror images of myself appeared. Always my physical body was in deep sleep. Then would my second body float into the dream. Then a third body might appear, instructing the second one. Then a fourth body might emerge, seeking another direction. There existed infinite dream bodies! Yet all were transparent and weightless. Never did a library book describe this phenomenon. Was the sixth sense perhaps more expansive than the limitations of physical form?

Most often, my second body directed these dreams. Spontaneous images would appear, then crystal clear light. My dream self would focus on the clearest image! Scenes would surface with unexpected turns, even parallel endings. My second body observed my other dream bodies choosing different paths. How agile were these transparent light forms, directing scenes to their satisfaction. Yet my physical energy seemed to sustain my ability to *see* these multiple images. The greater my strength, the more vivid the visions.

Before awakening from sleep, my mind would review what had happened during the night. This borderland space of twilight time held my dream memory. Here my thoughts imprinted the sixth sense upon my waking mind, documenting the dream. Never did I question from *where* these visions arose. The twilight zone was crystal clear. How this space bridged the psychic reality of the sixth sense with the physical reality of the five senses. Silver Dreams ceased to puzzle me. Did they not abound with multi-dimensional scenes, infinite voices, parallel universes? Memory that encompassed past, present, and future as one. Visions from boundless sources. Was the sixth sense not a psychic space, vast and limitless?

Yet the power to contact Silver Dreams came from my free will. The more sensitive my sixth sense, the more could I, Aisling, receive its wisdom. Why Night School instructions aboard the Silver Bubble were not strange at all! They were simply teachings about the sixth sense. No wonder beings appeared from everywhere imaginable. Were all not receiving multi-dimensional truths? Opening our minds to the clarity of crystal energy, unblocking negative vibrations from ancient myths. Creating a collective mind that was pure crystal light itself.

No longer did the Night School dream of Vivienne, as mysterious Queen Medusa, perplex my psyche. How she belonged besides the ugly Gorgon Medusa. Were they not mirror reflections seeking a balanced whole? Yet why had gallant Geraint appeared in that strange dream? Surely his story was incomplete, many clues missing. Suddenly, my mind went blank. Perhaps there was something I, Aisling, did not want to know. Closing the library book, my mind whirled. My eyes stared into space. Surely another spiral was about to begin.

Thinking only of Night School, my sight intensified. Surroundings dissolved. The library table faded away, books before me disappeared. The sixth sense encompassed my being. Then, although all was light and weightless, my five senses remained acute. My psyche could feel Vivienne slide into the seat next to mine. The sensation of her presence entered my awareness. My whole being felt Vivienne scanning the library books. My psychic perception was using six senses at once. Without stirring, my mind had discerned Vivienne as anxious. She was leafing hurriedly through the books.

Her tension became stronger than my tranquillity. My energy could not sustain my calm. "Aisling!" Vivienne cried, then covered her face with the broadest book. "I've got to talk with you! It's absolutely urgent!" As returning from the twilight zone of sleep, so my mind awoke from reverie. Yet instantly my awareness became alert. My astonishment met her fright. Vivienne's sea green eyes held a panic never seen before. Her urgency pleaded for a library corner where we could confide. "Maybe we can speak in the book stacks for a moment," my hushed voice replied, "Clearly we cannot talk here."

Vivienne followed my path. Pretending to be searching for poetry books, no one noticed us together. Her words burst out, "You, Aisling, were in my dream last night! Not only *in my dream* but on that bizarre Silver Bubble we once talked about. Geraint was there as well. And beings strange and senseless. Am I raving mad? How did this happen to me?" My astonished expression met her shock, my words became measured. "What do you think that mass of books is all about?" Then did my sentences stop for a moment. "What do you think I am reading? Why do you think I am searching through those pages? Trying to discover *what* is happening." Vivienne seemed frozen. "Vivienne!" I exclaimed, "I had the same dream. Only now my mind is beginning to understand what is happening."

The two of us stood still, staring at one another, stuck in silence.

Had he truly seen himself
as a medieval hero clothed in
crimson tunic and gold sandals?

· XVI ·
THE TIME
IS NOW

GERAINT'S TEMPLES WERE THROBBING, his head pounding. His dreams now flooded with dramas he neither understood nor wanted to interpret. Covering his black dishevelled hair with the crumpled pillow, he hid the coming daylight from his eyes. What seemed faraway memory still lingered in his thoughts. How last night's dream had frazzled his mind. Had he truly seen himself as a medieval hero clothed in crimson tunic and gold sandals? Just thinking the thought seemed absurd. And that blinding crystal screen, pulsating with transparent pictures. Strobe lights flashing scene after scene. It was all too ridiculous. Why Geraint even remembered a silver mermaid! Mesmerizing mirrors, curved and convoluted. And the gold sword frozen in a frame of ice, in a Crystal Castle beneath the silver sea.

How that flaming voice of Ruby Red still burned in his ear. Imagine! Someone luring his senses, enticing his passion and pride. Now what were the words that peculiar being had proclaimed? Were they not imprinted in his mind? How they resounded as an echo in space! Were the sentences not strange and somber:

Geraint, hero of the soul, extol yourself!

Reveal your charms and ancient grace
Let not another mortal take your place.
Awake your slow and sleeping thoughts
Or all past hopes will come to naught.

Remember times of prophecy and prose
When omens and oracles with clarity arose.
When body, speech, and mind did sound as one

91

And rainbow light embraced the fiery sun.

Then did deep waters consume your blazing heat
Forcing red flames of fire quickly to retreat.
Treacherous tides did shake the earth and every tree
Pulling *you* by silver threads beneath the silver sea.

There the hag whose wisdom eye is frozen still in fright
Holds tight your dreams, your horrors of the night.
The time is now to find your courage through this plight
For only you, Geraint, can change past wrongs to right.

Geraint was stunned by what he remembered. Surely this morning hour was too early to be distraught. How he detested confusion. And here was a situation neither logical nor rational. Suddenly he remembered Vivienne. Was that problem not on the agenda as well? Perhaps he could cover his head, withdraw beneath the bed covers, forget his fate. A chorus of serpents clamored from each tank. "Oh, no!" Geraint cried with exasperation, "Those hissing snakes again!" Geraint had never heard such clatter before. Covering his ears did not help. Throwing cold water on his sleepy face, he confronted his conscience.

Again did he approach the diamondback rattlesnake, meeting him eye to eye. Their conversation continued from before. Geraint heard himself say, "Is it a silver mermaid beneath the silver sea?" Then did negative hissing sounds retort loud and clear. Next he tried, "The forest of forgetfulness?" No reaction. Suddenly reluctant Geraint sparkled with, "Vivienne, the vixen?" Applause of approval met his cryptic comment. Standing in his wrinkled bathrobe, Geraint dramatized his decision! "Then onwards and upwards to victory!" he shouted to his snakes. Was he not waving an imaginary gold sword in the air? Had he gone berserk? Sensible Geraint saying such things. Had screws loosened in his head?

School that morning was an avoidance of Aisling and an allurement of Vivienne. Yet what made him so certain she would accept his advances? Confident, Geraint smiled to himself. His electric blue eyes would magnetize her. The question was *where* not *when*. His preferred time was late afternoon. Coffee and cake, saunter and stroll, some harmless seduction. Yet Geraint found himself agitated at school, anxious to follow her movements from hour to hour. By the time classes concluded, he was an internal wreck. Decidedly an indirect approach would be preferable.

"You interested in snakes?" he casually blurted at Vivienne as she slithered out the front school door. Turning in surprise, she simply replied, "Oh, it's you." Then did his direct approach catch her off guard. "No, seriously, I mean it. Thought your elusive ways could be enticed." Vivienne felt her sea green eyes flame. Abruptly did she answer him, "What do you know about snakes?" To which Geraint added, "Have coffee with me. Then you'll find out!" Vivienne looked suspicious! "No, don't want to be late for my appointment." "Fine," said persistent Geraint. "I'll walk with you, wherever you're going!" To her surprise, Vivienne agreed. Anyhow, she found him attractive in an anxious way.

Yet, walking towards the painter's studio, Vivienne hardly spoke. Geraint found himself creating conversation. His curiosity longed to know *where* she was going. As they reached her destination, Geraint offered his prize. "How about visiting me sometimes? Want to see my snake collection? Maybe you can converse with the diamondback rattlesnake!" Suddenly Vivienne realized Geraint was serious. Softening she said, "No, sorry, afternoons are taken. My portrait is being painted." Then did the heavens open. "How would you like a few snakes around your neck?" Geraint persevered. "Perhaps coiled around your arms? Maybe at your feet? They're tame, you know." Vivienne could not help but smile. In a peculiar way the idea appealed to her. "How would you manage that?" she taunted him. To which Geraint replied, "Tell me *when* and *where*. As many snakes as you wish shall be brought to the painter's studio!"

That's how it all began. When requested, Geraint would bring snakes into the studio. He would stay or leave, whichever pleased Vivienne. Yet she seemed not to consult the artist. Nor did they speak. Geraint felt peculiar, and the silence of the studio puzzled him. Yet the portrait proved more bizarre than the ambience. Before Geraint's astonished eyes, Vivienne emerged as a psychic Queen, mysterious and magical. A Kingdom under the Sea came to life. Strangest of all, the picture became a portrait within a portrait within a portrait. Here, Vivienne the Queen, was painting white roses into red poppies. Was the artist changing the white of chastity to the red of ecstasy? So Geraint liked to imagine.

"Vivienne!" Geraint would jeer, "What eternal beauty and perfection! The ultimate in silence and immortality. Such a splendid crown of silver stars upon your head." Vivienne relished the exaggeration. "Ah me!" she would say, "Snakes seeking a shining sword of gold. Might this sword of strength not cut through your illusion?" Undaunted, Geraint would continue. "Are you not the psychic Queen of life, source of all living things? Might the Milky Way, the serpent pathway in the sky, not be yours to travel?" Then would Vivienne pause. Her sea green eyes would ponder. "Take care, Geraint!" she would spitefully add, "The phoenix in my shield protects my soul enthroned in space!" To which Geraint would stoop and bow, proper conduct for a hero.

How the portrait intrigued Geraint. Slowly did he see Vivienne become passive and feminine. Her weapons feelings, not thoughts. Portrayed as an ethereal

93

beauty, she seemed imaginative, intuitive, intelligent. Why then was this Queen of Heaven surrounded by a sea of sorrow? Encased in frozen water, her beauty seemed solid as crystal ice itself. Yet the full moon covered her crown of twelve silver stars. Why had her power been petrified? How Geraint, the hero, thought to offer an immortal kiss! With love might the sorrowful Queen come to life again. "No doubt," thought he, "the artist thinks the same."

Yet his precious snakes were portrayed with poison. Venomous and violent, Geraint cringed from what he now beheld. How he took offense! Writhing serpents surrounded Vivienne's bejewelled feet. Crawling upon the floor, they prepared to strike whomever touched their Queen. Then had Vivienne's face changed from friend to foe. Geraint dared not look into her sea green eyes. Staring through silence into space, she refused to receive him! Yet something strong remained unresolved. Even his snakes at home, hovering in the dark green bedroom, became restless. What mystery still lingered? Suddenly Geraint remembered the silver mermaid. Might her silver mirror reveal Vivienne's connection to the Kingdom under the Sea? Yet how could he call upon this creature? Clearly, he preferred present trials to her temptations.

Then did strategy offer a solution. Geraint chose the forest of his fate rather than the sea of sorrow. Through the paths of silence he walked without protection of his snakes. The woodlands were veiled in twilight. A strange light filtered through branches of tall trees. Leaves began to quiver, and the earth trembled. Then did Geraint behold a serpent one hundred feet long, the color of lapis lazuli. Was it not inlaid with gold, surrounded by silver rays? Geraint knew this serpent was omnipotent enough to poison the stream from which it drank. Clearly it could kill anything with a glance. Might this not be the female Python he once had slain? Geraint heard tremors of strange winds through cool branches. Everything before his eyes began to float. Had he crossed into a space beyond his senses? Suddenly the bizarre became potent and plausible.

The dazzling stream turned into a river of Fire! Its brilliant hues of red, blue, and green nearly blinded his eyes. Salamanders seemed the only creatures who could live within. Geraint knew they thrived on invisible flames, without their vibrations fire could not exist. Without them there would be no warmth. Their radiant splendor caused continuous flames to burn. Yet their warning to Geraint was clear. "He who cannot curb his passions is a plaything for us." Feeling near faint from their heat, Geraint washed his face in the shimmering stream. Then did a strange voice call through the air. Startled, Geraint turned around, looked above.

"Well, are you not curious about my companions?" spoke an uncommon voice. Again did Geraint swerve around. Yet no other creatures were about. Straining his neck he beheld a beauteous bird, one who often appeared in his deepest

Then did Geraint behold a serpent one hundred feet long,
the color of lapis lazuli.

dreams. Reverent, Geraint felt privileged to be in its presence. "Too long have you been playing with fire!" spoke this curious creature. Geraint started to defend himself. Yet the magnificent bird insisted, "Do you not know to whom you are speaking?" Astonished, Geraint found himself flustered.

Then did the majestic bird proclaim, "Aisling knows me as Urag. For you Garu will do. Others call me Garuda, King of Heaven." Spreading his golden wings, he stared at Geraint with displeasure. Then he prepared to soar towards the sun. "Wait Garu! Wait!" cried Geraint. "You have not told me anything!" The majestic bird turned impatiently. "Do you not know yourself as Prince of Peace? The shining star from Heaven sent. Shot from the spiral of the Milky Way, path of the serpent in the sky." Without a moment for Geraint to reflect, Garu continued, "Why then have you spoken with creatures below the sea? Even made vows to Queen Agan, the Naga Queen of Serpent power. Such actions have displeased the most divine." Geraint cried out in confusion, "What wrong have I done?" Flapping his golden wings, Garu hesitated but a moment.

Suddenly his wings turned to bright sapphire, his ruby eyes became deep and dangerous. Once again did he speak, "Perhaps you might remember witches and wiles, darkness and disgrace, power and punishment. All this must be unveiled before peace is possible." Lest Geraint become discouraged, with a quick wink he hinted, "The Kingdom of dreams receives those predestined for the path. Chosen by birth or by fate, your choices are the myth that you create." Geraint realized that witches and wiles, darkness and disgrace, power and punishment were what first frightened him about Vivienne. Chills raced through his body.

Was his memory not mocking him? Was his vision not *seeing* Vivienne, the mystical Queen, transformed into someone wrinkled, ancient as eternity? Older than time, vaster than space, so deadly that men appeared and disappeared before her eyes. Then did Geraint sense another personality. He *saw* Vivienne as vain and self-righteous, with a sharp tongue that could not be trusted. A female who took offence over imagined wrongs, who did not tell the entire truth. Had Vivienne not reminded him of a snake, striking but meaning no harm? Had she not been devious, every sentence part fiction? Her beauty was capable of bringing destruction, her sea green eyes lured men into idle fantasies. Clearly her opulence had made him more than nervous.

Was Geraint not seeing her negative side? The darkness of her shadow-self. That part which provoked criticism and reproach. Had Vivienne not been suspicious of things not understood? Her distant manner forbidding another to approach. Yet might this not be a mask, protecting some hidden power? How often Geraint had found her words meaningless! Her loyalties changing with her mood, her psyche rejecting emotions, suppressing all desires. How her sea green eyes would hiss like a snake, preventing another from touching her. Then did denied feelings strike with a

95

force strong enough to turn Geraint to stone.

To understand this dilemma was his deepest desire. Yet hidden emotions lay buried beneath the waters. Was he not being lured again to the Kingdom under the Sea? Need he again encounter the Naga Queen Agan? How his head swam with meaningless solutions! Nothing seemed right. Might his psyche be preparing him to proceed alone? To enter the forest of fate, there to await the destiny of a hero. Then did he remember the salamander with its invisible fire. Geraint could carry a flaming torch wherever he went. He could burn to ashes whatever challenged his command. He could pass through rings of smoke and flame. In that instant of decision Geraint *saw* flaming balls of light, red tongues of fire. The last thing he recalled were his thoughts consumed by warmth. Walking through heat he could feel candle flames encircling a Palace of Ice. Had he not long ago *seen* such a palace transformed into a Crystal Castle?

Perhaps his imagination was playing tricks again. Exhausted, Geraint sank into himself, wondering what the woodlands would offer next.

*Why there was a lock-keeper's cottage,
covered with climbing red roses
in full bloom!*

· XVII ·
PROUD
PEGASUS

APTAIN NODI FELT FINE ABOUT THE SE-
QUENCE OF EVENTS. Most things were happening
as planned, yet now the time had come for Aisling
to return to the boat Nebulae. With haste did he prepare the narrow boat, brass
polished until it glistened. Lace curtains inside the boatman's cabin were washed
and ironed. Chimney stacks cleaned until smoke lifted straight into the windless
air. Paint work was mopped down. Then there was paraffin for the hurricane lamps,
a sack of coal for the stove, water for the buckby can. As the narrow boat rocked on
the water, so its ribbon plates tinkled with a celestial music of their own. Captain
Nodi, pleased with himself, then considered a sea voyage by way of the canal.

Through brass portholes he watched the breeze ruffled waters. Sunlight,
weaving patterns of shifting light, flickered across the cabin ceiling. Slowly did he
fill the black painted bucket with coal, prepare the stove. Then his mind stretched
to see *where* Aisling might be found. Ah, there she was before the fire, huddled over
books again, trying to figure things out. So Captain Nodi decided to deceive her.
Thought to cast a common spell. He would help her fall asleep before the open
pages. Then would she awaken in his arms, his forever more. "No, no, no!" he muttered to himself, "None of that rubbish will do! Long gone is that scenario!" Thus
he made himself reconsider his furtive plans.

Stepping above deck, slippery Captain Nodi prepared the elum tiller for
Aisling's arrival. He reminded himself that the steerer was the one who worked the
tiller. That its tall rudder post, painted as a barber's pole, was called a ram's head. Yet
how much more need Aisling know? What he really wanted was for her to call him
"Number One," the proper name for the captain owner of a narrow boat. Yet how
could he demand such respect without earning it? Then, pensively, Captain Nodi
placed a fender of plaited rope above the ram's head. Would his favorite horse's tail

not bring good luck? Was it not a remembrance of devoted service? How well he could hear the old creak of its tackle! The steady clip-clop of its hooves on the tow-path.

The present pattern was far from perfect. Disobedient was his nowadays horse, its flighty temperament soaring with the winds, its rebellious rage beyond control. Yet Captain Nodi knew that Susagep came from immortal blood. Had *fate* not brought them together again? Slowly did Captain Nodi evaluate the present situation. Then did he harness Susagep with shining leather, adorned with ornaments of glittering brass. Reflective, Number One plaited bright red ribbons through its mane, filled its feed bucket with hay and oats. Red and blue tufts were placed around its ankles. Captain Nodi brushed Susagep's straggly hair until it reached the ground. As father to an errant son, so he both admired his offspring and wished to send him on his way.

As usual, everything became more complicated than calm. Then did Captain Nodi decide to take another look. So he reassured himself, "Yes, everything is going just fine." Slowly he washed his old chipped cup, lit the stove, began to brew fresh coffee. Then he recalled that lemon tea lifted Aisling's spirits, made her feel at home. As the whistling kettle boiled, so his mind drifted to the faraway scene. Yes, Aisling's father had found her asleep, did not disturb her peace. Telepathic thoughts made him place another log upon the fire's flames. Surely its warmth would lure Aisling to deeper realms. For a moment did her father hesitate, then silently he shut the library door behind him. Clearly his daughter's mind was already beyond present time.

Summoned by Number One himself, dreaming Aisling heard the rumbling engine start. Water, on the kitchen stove, seemed forever boiling. Then she spotted the teapot steaming with lemon scent, honey and biscuits by its side. Yet was Nebulae not travelling through waters unknown? No longer was the narrow boat tied to the shore, it seemed lost on a far and lonely waterway. Slowly meandering the still course of the canal, the absolute silence of the air was unbroken. Even the rustle of wind in the reeds had died. Something ominous made Aisling uneasy.

"Welcome aboard!" Captain Nodi shouted through the boatman's cabin door. Steering Nebulae towards a distant lock, Aisling noticed the engine noise had ceased. "How about leading our horse along the tow-path?" his voice bellowed again. Clearly Captain Nodi did not want Aisling to be lost in a dream. "What horse are you talking about?" she asked perplexed. Captain Nodi replied, already exasperated, "That one, my dear! The one on the tow-path! The shaggy horse waiting to tow us towards the locks!" Aisling could not believe her eyes. That ridiculous creature pulled the boat along? That bedecked beast tied to the front of the Nebulae? Why his tow-line was slack upon the muddy banks. Not waiting for her usual comment, Captain Nodi called again, "His name is Susagep. Just call him Susa. Susa will be fine." Then he prepared the gang-plank for Aisling to reach the shore.

Yet how foolish could she be? Aisling was trying to mount the horse. "No! Not yet! Here no one rides Susagep!" cried Captain Nodi, his patience peaked. "Just take his reins. Lead him along the tow-path." Yet the horse knew more than Aisling. Tightly did she cling to his reins! How the leather hurt the palms of her hands. Yet, in an instant, they were upon the bridge before the lock. Again, Captain Nodi was calling loud and clear, "Take him across the arched bridge. Susa needs help with the steps." Once across, Number One eased the boat to the shore. Then he tied Nebulae to the nearest tree. "Now, come aboard, and have some lemon tea," he shouted to his helper.

From the upper deck Aisling could see the distant scene. Why there was a lock-keeper's cottage, covered with climbing red roses in full bloom. White jasmine clustered about its windows filling the air with fragrance. As the lock-keeper appeared, he exclaimed, "Welcome to Number One! Captain of Nebulae! Have you had a good day? Aye, as delicious as your night?" To which Captain Nodi returned a twinkling eye, a smile that savored a thought. Embarrassed, he turned to Aisling and explained. "Lock-keepers have a solitary life, away from villages, even roads. They do fancy gossiping when a boat comes along." When Captain Nodi joined the lock-keeper ashore, they bantered some more in the one-room store near the lock. Purchasing licorice bootlaces and sherbet suckers, he hoped to appease Aisling of the dream. Then he stopped and patted patient Susa. Suddenly, Captain Nodi turned around.

To the lock-keeper's surprise, he offered an invitation. "Come meet Aisling, my starry-eyed friend!" Captain Nodi coyly announced. Then he asked a favor of his old friend. "Could she help open the paddle locks? With my windlass, of course." The lock-keeper stood startled. Never before had Captain Nodi given his windlass to another. Aisling had already noticed the lock paddles. The ancient gates were so heavy only men could turn their crank. And the cavernous walls of the lock, did they not rise high above Nebulae's deck? Clearly its wet bricks left only inches to spare on either side. Captain Nodi had thrust the windlass into her hand. Was he not holding the tiller straight, keeping Nebulae from swinging side to side? Already the first heavy lock-gates had been opened. Slowly did Number One ease the narrow boat within. Next these paddle locks needed to be closed. "Aisling!" he instructed, "Carefully climb the ladder on the lock wall. The lock-keeper waits above." Her frightened feet barely reached the ladder's iron rung. As Captain Nodi watched her ascend the wall, he shouted from below. "Keep the windlass safe. Tuck it inside your belt." Petrified, Aisling could hardly believe her plight.

Night stars were beginning to appear. Captain Nodi lighted the oil lamps, their beams would brighten the second paddle gates. Cautiously the lock-keeper guided Aisling across the rotting wooden beams. Cranking the windlass through its paddle ratchets, so he freed the right lock paddle. Then he instructed Aisling to do

99

the same on the other side. Frightened, Aisling had to cross the wooden lock beam. Clutching the windlass, she prepared to wind the farthest paddle. Captain Nodi held the tiller tight, awaiting the coming rush of water. When the waters entered the lock, the narrow boat swayed from side to side, as Nebulae rose several feet higher.

The light from the headlamp silhouetted her shape. Suddenly there was a rattle and a clang. "First catch must have slipped," he thought. Aisling was bending over the paddle gear on the towpath side. Was she not trying to place the catch in position? Captain Nodi chuckled to himself. Slowly and steadily she cranked up the paddle. Then he wondered why the lock-keeper had disappeared from sight. "Oh well," he muttered to himself. Aisling was checking the catch again. Then she crossed the rotting wooden beam to rewind the first paddle. As she reached the far side, a fierce rattling sound broke through the night as the second paddle hurtled back into place.

"What's the matter with the catches?" hollered Captain Nodi. Clambering to the cabin roof, he hoped for a better view. "Can't understand why they keep slipping," Aisling shouted, "Do you want me to try again?" Desperately, four times did she turn the windlass around each paddle. Yet as Aisling crossed the rotting beams, the paddle dropped again. "Come back," Captain Nodi called, "Clearly we cannot get through." Once more he bellowed, "Get the tow-rope from Susa. Then throw it down to me, he'll hold Nebulae in place." But the dark night played tricks with her vision. In the shadows of the lock shapes suddenly appeared, then vanished. Had the lock paddles been a fantasy trick? No matter how Aisling wound them, they slipped again when she moved away.

The silence of the night seemed fraught with fear. Frantic, Aisling called down to Captain Nodi. "My hands hurt, my fingers are cold. After Susa is tied, then what shall I do? Where must we go?" To which he calmly replied, "Why, Aisling, we must dive under the sea, of course!" Lest she think him jesting, hastily he added, "Now quickly, Aisling, mount Susagep. Ask no questions! Clasp your arms around his neck. Pronounce RETAW and hold tight." Instantly did the horse Susa buck, nearly hurling Aisling into the deep water of the lock. Captain Nodi continued unabated! "Now tell Susagep that ERISED calls for his cooperation. That RORRIM knows what he needs to see." Before Aisling realized Captain Nodi knew these names, the dark water turned into whirlpools of foam. Clutching onto Susa, she found herself diving into eddies, swirling in circles and spirals.

Once beneath these waters, the tow-rope became braided red and white ribbons. What had been a shaggy Susa now seemed a white winged horse, wearing a golden bridle. Vibrations began to shift! Suddenly, the sluggish horse arose with radiant energy. Now rebellious white wings commanded the powers of Susa's mind. What had been indolent now moved with speed. What had been slow was spirited.

Yet something strange had penetrated the horse's mind. Some curious competition had come about. Why were Susagep and Captain Nodi at odds with one another?

Aisling needed to question Number One, who instead of steering the tiller was standing with a silver trident in hand. She found herself screaming in despair, "Help me! Where are we going? What's happening?" Yet, as waters turned turquoise and emerald green, Susa's white wings spread as rushing winds. Once more did Captain Nodi take command. "Look for the candle lights," he shouted, "Their flames must find us in these darkened waters." Then did Susagep hasten onwards. Anxiously Aisling stroked its mane, proclaimed excited words! "Soon shall your inspiration soar!" she heard herself exclaim. "Your wings of creativity will be free. Heavenly realms shall touch the Earth, while Earth shall reach towards Heaven." Aisling was shocked to speak such lofty words, and even the white winged horse whinnied in surprise. Then more bizarre thoughts flashed through her mind:

When Susa's name will you *see*
Then shall Susagep be free!

The sea water turned to purple black! In this darkness, Aisling lost her *sense* but not her *sight*. Yet, in a strange second of truth, another vision pierced her mind. Then did she laugh aloud, "Why you are not Susagep but Pegasus himself! Flying clear as clouds, are you not the white winged horse of inspiration?" Silence made her say even more. "Of course, Pegasus, the offspring of Poseidon and Medusa. That's who you are!" Released at last, his golden bridle glistening with delight, Pegasus wished to take quick flight. But Aisling stopped this tempting trip. "Shame on you!" she said, "To desert me in my dreams." Then did Aisling add with curiosity, "Now tell me, Pegasus, whom do you pursue? Mad Medusa? The mystical Gorgon Queen herself?" Pegasus, so pleased, replied, "Why these strange truths remain for you to find!" Abruptly did he accelerate, and Aisling clutched him even closer!

"Aisling, concentrate on the flaming candles!" Captain Nodi shouted anew. Then, pointing his silver trident, did he plague Pegasus. "From my waters of emotion flow your divine revelation and inspiration." Yet rebellious Pegasus paid him no heed. Captain Nodi raged and stormed! "What does it matter who wins? A son must honor his father, forgive his sins." To which proud Pegasus replied, "Does your illusion speak this as a truth?" Aisling could hardly believe her ears. She chose to withdraw, to not comprehend this conversation. Clearly she wished not to be involved.

Suddenly her mind heard a female voice, wailing from the darkened waters. With compassion and concern Aisling heeded its plea. Was the voice not chanting a strange song?

101

Silver circles turn you round,
Silver circles touch my crown.
Take you through the waters deep,
End my years of frozen sleep.

Help my eyes to open wide,
Cast my wonder not aside.
Breathe into the heart of flame,
Precious gifts to make me sane.

Help my mind to daylight *see*,
Return again the wisdom tree.
Awaken memory of each night,
Release the darkness of my *sight*.

Hearing the wailing voice, Captain Nodi cringed with shame. Pegasus searched for this song of sadness. Yet what forces were fighting in this sea of sorrows? Desperately, Aisling tried to look through these deep waters. Where were the candle flames? How Pegasus pulled in one direction, Captain Nodi steering Nebulae in another. "Stop! Stop!" her courageous voice cried. "Are we to drown in these raging waters? Are we not in this drama together?" Then did Pegasus raise his lowered head. Captain Nodi straightened the tiller. In that moment of recognition, three faint candles flickered in the distance. Then many lights formed a path, to ease their perilous passage.

Yet everything seemed to be changing at once. Caught at the crossroad, how Aisling considered choices other than going forward. Yet, looking backward, the saga ceased. Faintly could she hear her father's voice. "Aisling! Aisling!" he was calling. "It's dinner time! Wake up!" As her eyes slowly lifted, three flames in the dying embers suddenly flared. Then did they fade from sight. Still immersed in the sea, Aisling tried to sleep again. Yet Father was persistent. "Wake up Aisling! Mother is waiting! Dinner is being served!" Trying to return, her mind split into fragments. Wanting to connect everywhere, she felt torn by parallel dimensions.

Slowly did her body stretch and awaken. Yet Aisling resented returning. Her agitated thoughts continued, "Why aren't my mind and body *ever* in the same place?"

*Captain Nodi, pleased with himself, then considered a sea voyage
by way of the canal.*

"Tell me Captain Nodi," she anxiously asked,
"What turned Medusa mad?"

· XVIII ·

CRYSTAL
CLARITY

QUEEN AGAN HAD WAITED AN ETERNITY. No longer need she keep her silence for at last the long awaited actions were taking place. Had her dreams not foretold these events? Three days had her silver mermaids burned frankincense and myrrh. As the incense was removed, its vibrations lingered in the ceremonial chamber. How carefully had these scents been selected. Did they not stimulate memory, activate inner perception? Having been properly prepared, parallel lives could now be invoked. Energies, needing to be seen, soon would reawaken. Passageways would open to coinciding worlds. Now would Queen Agan watch Aisling and Captain Nodi arrive. Had twilight time not come?

Yet neither Aisling nor Captain Nodi fathomed how they had chosen this space. Why were they within a ceremonial chamber, silver mermaids anointing them with aromatic oils of hyacinth and gardenia? Unforeseen, they were sitting in stillness. Then the vibrations in the chamber slowly rose! Serpents were rotating in a counterclockwise coil. One hundred and forty-four times had they spun this spiral. Aisling and Captain Nodi began to drift away. Suddenly, from the center of this whirling vortex, Queen Agan appeared. Yet hardly did she greet her guests.

"Focus your eyes," the Serpent Queen commanded, "Our vibrations must journey to a specific place, a precise time, through another way of *seeing*." Then did concern fill the ceremonial chamber. "To where are we voyaging?" asked Aisling, most anxious. "To the scene where mad Medusa was slain!" declared psychic Queen Agan. "Should that be your wish," Captain Nodi spoke, "then shall my rightful name be proclaimed. How well you know Medusa never heard of Nodiesop. How often did she call forth Poseidon, ruler of the sea, creator of storms, love of her life! Had not proud Poseidon sired their immortal offspring?"

Aisling was beyond comment. Already out of her body, her shadow had

103

coupled with the vibrations of mad Medusa. Was she not experiencing the sensation of petrifying men to stone? Yet *what* in them had died when staring into mad Medusa's eyes? Aisling turned to Captain Nodi for an explanation. Surely something in his magnificence once made Medusa meek. Some secret which he never shared. "Tell me Captain Nodi," she anxiously asked, "What turned Medusa mad?" "Ah!" pondered the Captain. "Illusion, of course, my dear!" Aisling did not understand. "After the chase for her chastity so came the capture," he attempted to explain. "And, when the capture was complete, like many men, Poseidon sought another." Then he stared into this time and place. "How mystical Queen Medusa once enchanted me! How well we pleasured one another in Athena's sacred temple. Now let me recall, had she enticed me? Had Poseidon taken her by surprise? No matter! Mysterious Queen Medusa angered the goddess Athena twice. She claimed herself more beauteous, and she savored sensual love before her sacred shrine. Was the second not the final storm?"

Then did Captain Nodi take a deep breath, permitting remorse to release itself. How well Queen Agan knew that mortal Queen Medusa was then cursed! Her ravishing hair turned to writhing snakes, her lovely eyes soon lonely with despair. Her wrath now petrifying men to stone. Memory made Captain Nodi speak with measured sadness. "Since then my sea-faring eyes have not beheld the enchanting Gorgon Queen." Aisling was aghast. "Yet did your heart not betray her soul? Did your power do nothing to protect her pain?" Aisling felt compassion for the dark shadow of Medusa's pride. Had her deceit not consumed her delightful side? Had vengeful Athena not sent poisonous serpents to prevent her seduction of men? Never would lust look directly into her sea green eyes again. Yet did mad Medusa not reflect the terror each man held within?

Turning to Captain Nodi, Queen Agan spoke again. "Shall the dignity and grace of Medusa not be restored? The Gorgon Queen who knew secrets of beauty, wisdom, immortality. Surely you agree that avoidance created endless anxiety." Still Queen Agan would not cease. "Was Medusa not a Queen of dreams, offering inspiration and intuition? Yet you, Captain Nodi, chose not to defend creation and creativity. Thus your offspring had to teach you this. Did proud Pegasus not bring forth inspiration? Did Chrysaor's sword of gold not cut through all illusion?"

Captain Nodi paused before he spoke again. "From your truth, Queen Agan, this seems correct. My way need not defend itself. The past, however, provokes you in present time. Clearly some changes now must come." With caution did the Queen of Serpents speak. "The emotions of Medusa are frozen as a block of ice. Yet is she not a triple goddess, a Gorgon Queen protecting sacred psychic secrets? Her intuition must be honored again. Tonight must we restore *sight* to the beheaded one. The clarity of Medusa must *say* what others dare not *see*." Aisling sat in shock, as the Serpent Queen continued. "Without such sensitivity, the jewel of sight turns to solid stone. Then does the shadow of the soul fill with sadness. Yet we speak no blame. Only the right to begin again."

Silence spread across the surrounding space, and Aisling found herself back at the narrow boat Nebulae. Once again she was astride proud Pegasus. Only now, mad Medusa was leading them through torrential tides. "Where are we going?" Aisling shouted in her strongest voice. Yet her mind knew the answer. Somewhere, someplace, somehow, this scene was happening again. Would parallel dreams never cease? Would candle light not always flicker in the distance, the Crystal Castle forever surrounded by flames?

Yet why was this fiery light causing such confusion? How mad Medusa was spinning to the right, following the rhythm of the clock! Frantically did Aisling holler, "No, no, mad Medusa! You must circle the other way, against time itself! In the center of this vortex awaits the entrance to the sixth sense!" Yet Medusa would not listen. Only exhaustion made her surrender. Then gently did words sound, "Come, mournful Medusa. Are you not frazzled from all these years of pain? Come, rest in the narrow boat Nebulae. There shall we create a plan."

Captain Nodi stood before the painted double door, roses and castles in his hands. Cautiously mad Medusa entered the boatman's cabin. With compassion did he speak. "Oh, Queen Medusa, how many men have you punished because of lust and love? How your pride did not permit psychic powers to protect you. Instead, your *sight* turned men to stone and sadness." Then did Aisling feel this flash of truth. Yet Captain Nodi persisted. "Oh, beauteous one, had your intuition been honored, your soul would have been saved. How I loved the sea green eyes of Queen Medusa, her laughter and charm. Surely such traits would never bring another harm." Slowly did mad Medusa relinquish her rage. Then did she turn her weary eyes to a luminous maiden shining with light.

Suddenly Aisling found herself in Night School of the Silver Dream. She was standing before a dazzling mirror screen, beside Diamond White. Were both not staring at this shimmering screen? Watching the words of RORRIM, ERISED, RETAW sparkle before their *sight*. With apprehension did Aisling await the coming vision. Then, in the blink of an eye, the letters turned upon themselves. Why, instead of RORRIM, the word MIRROR blazed across the brilliant screen. Then did a familiar voice softly speak:

Aisling! Here appears the MIRROR of your dreams.
All hidden things that now you wish to glean.
Yet truth becomes what you perceive within.
No difference rests between the sacred and a sin.

How MIRRORS reveal wisdom for your eyes to behold!
Eternal reflections which are ready to be told.
Judge not what appears before your precious *sight*.
Know that each image holds both wrong and right.

Hardly had Aisling absorbed this scene when ERISED flashed across the
dazzling screen. In reverse it read as DESIRE!

Did DESIRE not lead you here today?
Did curiosity not entice you on the way?

DESIRES are temptations to force you into doubt.
To show that endless choices are the only route.

Then did RETAW burst across the brilliant screen. Shimmering with
shadows of Poseidon and the Serpent Queen Agan, clearly RETAW would change
to WATER.

How from WATERS of emotion, Aisling, you have come!
To receive compassion from the moon, clarity of the sun.
Now bring forth mad Medusa, Gorgon Queen of *sight*,
Then sunshine from Geraint shall make your life so bright.

Suddenly the mirror screen turned crystal clear. And who should appear in
heavenly blue with silver stars, but Vivienne with the full moon shining above her
ravishing hair. But why was she calling Geraint? He was in flaming red, standing
with the gold sword of Chrysaor by his side. "You must prove you are sincere!"
came her wanton words, "Then nothing need you ever fear!" Geraint the hero, taken
aback, suddenly found his heart. Was he ready to honor her request? How Vivienne
continued with care and concern! "Soon twilight time shall lift the veil, then may
you penetrate the Palace of Ice. There, two cauldrons await to challenge your determination. Here must you survive alive or forever shall you burn!" Geraint heeded
his destiny! Intuitively Vivienne continued to converse, "Geraint make haste! Only
you can destroy the darkness of this night. Go forward with your might! Before dawn
must the Palace of Ice be changed into a Crystal Castle glowing with eternal light."
As everything turned pitch black, Aisling could vaguely *see* the shadow of
that strange bird Urag. Why had he suddenly appeared? Surely Geraint was calling
him Garu. Behind them appeared the name NIATNUOM. Garu was commanding

Geraint, speaking with the voice of destiny! "The MOUNTAIN reaches high for those who climb. Yet you may choose whatever size or shape you seek." So heeding, Geraint considered the cauldrons awaiting him. He thought these lesser mountains to overcome. Yet fate proved ferocious. Was not the first a cauldron of pure water, with vibrations to burn his flesh? Was not the second cauldron of hot dew, with energy penetrating enough to obliterate both body and bones? Was the Palace of Ice not heated with ruby wine scented with the aroma of cinnamon, strong enough to make him sleep for eternity?

Then did Geraint ordain that heavenly blue would help his visions arise as if in sleep. Bravely did he inhale its perfumes, receive the nectar of Paradise. How these sweet scents made his head light. Suddenly did Geraint *see* that past, present, and future exist in parallel time. Why everything was reflected in multi-mirrors of many minds. Was he not now experiencing only part of that precious picture? Surely he had provoked these obstacles to present themselves again. Yet why did he need barriers to find his beliefs? Clearly, whatever awaited in darkness, Geraint had not brought to the light of day.

"From questions come all answers!" greeted the golden voice of Garu. Again did Geraint inhale the sweet perfume of ruby wine scented with the aroma of cinnamon. Intending to cleanse his soul, slowly he stepped into the cauldron of pure water. Mad Medusa and her vicious snakes coiled around his mind! Their penetrating poison forcing his first vision to arise. Before his fearful mind stood Ruby Red, flashing sparks of fire. Bursting with flaming light, Geraint gathered strength and sensitivity. With blessings did he protect the perilous snakes. Never had he honored those who tried to poison him. Had the intensity of red hot flames melted his anxiety? Had compassion not calmed his soul?

"You have another tub to go!" called Garu, "Go with caution! Here vibrations are more concentrated. The cauldron more intense." The tub of hot mist, from which he intended to arise, forced Geraint to change. Its ember heat penetrated his psyche! Instantly, his negativity was purified and melted into vapor. Yet, without this energy, drowsing Geraint lingered longer than needed. As the sweet scents of red wine enticed him to sleep, so Garu shouted, "Leave! Lest you drown in indulgence!" Heeding these words, Geraint's blue eyes opened.

His *sight* was crystal clear! Was that not the golden sword of Chrysaor, frozen in a block of ice? Was mysterious Queen Medusa not immobile on her serpent throne? With the power of clear vision, Geraint focused on the golden sword. Rays of heat emanated from his penetrating eyes. As ice melted from his mind, so with clarity did Geraint clutch the golden sword of Chrysaor. With both hands he cut the cords of illusion that wound around this myth. Petrified Medusa with ruby red eyes transformed in twilight time. Writhing snakes returned to ravishing hair. The psychic *sight* of her soul no longer turned men to stone. Had Geraint not faced the truth behind illusion? Had the clarity in his eyes not met the clairvoyance in hers? Surely he had honored the one who ruled from the sixth sense. The negative *sight* of mad Medusa had been faced. Clearly the scourge of mad Medusa, the pride of Queen Medusa, had been cleansed by clarity. Now might Geraint return the sixth sense to its rightful throne.

As purple spider webs dissolved, sunlight surrounded mortal Queen Medusa. Shadows light and dark, creative and destructive, merged together. Mad Medusa and the mortal Queen, no longer mirror images, integrated the power of their *sight*. Once again did the Palace of Ice become the Crystal Castle. How the light of Ruby Red now blazed, lucid as the morning sun! Out from the sea of darkness sparkled the dazzling mirror screen. Diamond White reflected crystal stars and pulsating beams of light. Yet no more visions were to be seen. As Aisling realized her dream body had slipped into her physical body, Night School faded from sight. Yet one thought lingered in her sleepy mind. How did the sixth sense of *sight* connect her to the hero of her dreams?

108

Slowly did they fuse with glistening gold serpents
in the pathway of the sky.

· XIX ·

MOONLIGHT AND SUNSHINE

GERAINT WAS NO LONGER AFRAID OF HIS FEELINGS. The winds of change had blown through his mind. The destructive and creative psyche of Medusa had merged. Vivienne ceased to threaten him, and he no longer feared Aisling. Instead, Geraint *saw* her as never before. Yet some subtle energy lingered. He needed to know *why* Aisling seemed so mysterious, calm, impenetrable. Something about her remained intangible. Her silence, held within her thoughts, somehow said, "Are you willing to acknowledge your intuition?" Then another sentence would add, "To seek is to know. To dare is to wait. To *see* is to care."

Yet Aisling remained distant. Geraint found her silent and sensitive, pensive and psychic. Only now he understood *how* she listened to the vibrations hidden behind appearances. Dark and mysterious, clearly her tunnel vision penetrated many depths. Something about her energy incited the magician in him. In her presence, Geraint felt inspired to change through inner strength. Her vibrations excited the fire he held within. What about Aisling motivated him towards the mystery of herbs and healing, to the magic of stones and jewels? How had her psychic sensitivity awakened those qualities in him?

Thus it happened that one strange Saturday afternoon Geraint was drawn towards the river bank. Never had he gone in this direction before. Deep in thought, he walked several silent hours. How bizarre he felt when a clanging bell from a passing boat attracted his attention. Yet had he not seen this narrow boat in his dreams? Then a commanding voice made him turn his head. "Hello there!" the Captain called, "Would you help me bring our narrow boat to shore? All my helpers are asleep." "Sure," answered Geraint, surprised others were sleeping at this time of day. "What can I do for you?" To which the Captain instructed, "First pull the front rope. Bring the narrow boat to shore. Then wind the rope around the nearest tree.

After that do the same at the stern." Watching with amusement, Captain Nodi relished the moment. "Many thanks, young man! How about coming aboard for a spot of tea?" Noticing the narrow boat was called the Nebulae, Geraint thought "a cluster of stars" seemed the right name.

Yet what awaited within? Why, there was Garu, his head tucked beneath his sapphire wings, sound asleep in a glistening cage of shining brass. And who should be curled up on cushions, also deep in slumber? None other than Aisling! Geraint was too stunned to speak. Captain Nodi seized the moment. "You know these persons?" he swiftly asked. To which Geraint replied, "How do you know them?" A sinful smile answered with a smirk. "They are my oldest friends! And you?" Geraint, suspicious, suddenly began stumbling as from a dream. "Why, you were once Poseidon, God of seas and storms! Swain of the Gorgon Queen Medusa! Father of Pegasus and Chrysaor!" To which Captain Nodi, (also Poseidon and Number One,) belly laughed so loud that Aisling stirred from sleep.

She had been dreaming of Geraint. Seeing him as a magician playing with jewels and stones, transforming a golden sword into a crystal wand. Had its vibrations not touched the Earth, then reached the heights of Heaven? A crystal wand bringing mystery to the meaning of life, to the secrets of herbs and healing. Geraint was proposing to tame the chaos of experience. Was he not creating plans with a purpose, directing energy in dynamic ways? Geraint was proposing new directions to discover, claiming his crystal wand could open gates to the unconscious. Yet Aisling in the dream had clearly asked, "What do you want of me?" To which Geraint in the dream had rapidly replied, "Why to begin the beginning! To propose a path together!" Only then did serpentine snakes appear before her eyes, silver sea serpents spiralling towards the Milky Way. Slowly did they fuse with glistening gold serpents in the pathway of the sky. Aisling in the dream began to enter their cosmic energy.

The belly laugh of Captain Nodi had shocked her from sleep. Hardly had her eyes opened when, again, she was stunned in surprise. Her astonished voice exclaimed, "What are you doing here?" To which Geraint replied, "And the same for you!" Only the starkness of silence ensued. Thoughts suddenly seemed to slip away. Number One cheerfully called, "Anyone for a cup of tea?" His nervousness started to belly laugh aloud, shaking the golden cage. Annoyed, Garu woke from sleep. "Oh," his sunshine eyes sneered, "So you have arrived! Seeking your salvation?" Dumbfounded, Geraint knew less to do than to say. Taking a deep breath, suddenly the audacity of a hero arose. All the craft of a magician came forth. Indignant, Geraint demanded an explanation.

Then did Number One stop pouring tea and calmly turn to the center of the cabin. Attempting to smooth the situation, carefully he chose his words. "Neither of you know any more than the other!" He paused while silence penetrated the cozy

*As ice melted from his mind, so with clarity did Geraint clutch
the golden sword of Chrysaor.*

cabin. Then Number One continued to confess. "Listen carefully to my measured words!" he intensely spoke. "Aisling, you belong to the silver light of the Moon. Do you recall the vibrations of Diamond White? Were they not the psychic energy of intuition, imagination, insight?" He paused for a precious moment. "You, Geraint, come from the strength of the Sun. Did not the rays of Ruby Red resonate with rational logic and reason?" Captain Nodi turned towards the blackened stove, pretending to prepare fresh tea. Through the silence another voice spoke. Now Garu was heard. "And so Garuda of Heaven and Poseidon of the Sea decided to bring you together. Yet our intentions were not to speak of our attentions." Swiftly did Captain Nodi turn around and smile. "Yet how this myth became a mirror with many meanings!" Garuda flapped his golden wings, ready to declare peace. "Before the secrets of healing could unfold, did a psychic tale not need to be told? And so many shadows of the psyche were exposed. Has our myth of the sixth sense not clarified your *sight*?"

Yet, before any answer could arise, the narrow boat began spinning in a double spiral, and they were shooting into space. Aisling and Geraint falling from the sky, Nebulae vanishing into a cluster of distant stars! Had they not tumbled onto emerald grass before the calm waters of the canal? Surely what had seemed a dream clearly returned as reality! Yet how long had they been talking with one another? Sharing stories about snakes, shining jewels, and petrified stone. Speaking of the serpent Queen Agan. Suddenly Geraint was revealing his birthday vow. Telling about seeking a prophetess with *sight*, a female with intuition and imagination. Was Aisling not speaking of her remembrance of psychic secrets?

Then did they realize how Vivienne had woven them together. How mad Medusa and the Gorgon Queen had forced their shadows into light. Yet what of the others they had met? Night School on the Silver Bubble? Would their Silver Dreams now cease? As shadows of twilight fell upon the emerald grass, behind Geraint appeared Ruby Red and the golden Garuda. Next to Aisling stood Diamond White, with Poseidon and Queen Agan on either side.

Aisling fell asleep by the light of the Moon, Geraint slumbered from the heat of the Sun. It mattered not *where* or *when* or *why* or *what* would happen next. Peace had begun between them. Were they both not under a blanket of brightness? Were they each not protected by a cluster of stars called Nebulae? A parallel galaxy that knew everything and everyone at once. An existence that existed before and even now.

Their mutual sleep was light as a breeze, deep as any depth. Yet calming thoughts drifted from what seemed long ago, and maybe even tomorrow. Did Aisling hear the whisper of a Silver Bird? How tenderly it was calling, "Trusting is not knowing where you are going! And faith is the path of the heart!" Then did Queen Agan softly say, "Was Medusa not a Queen of dreams, offering inspiration and intuition?" While Geraint, dreaming of flying, *seeing* flapping golden wings, heard his majestic friend say, "From questions come all answers!" As each fell into a deeper sleep, they dreamed the same dream about their mutual destiny.

112